The Lotus Blossom Chronicles
by
Jax Cassidy
Simone Harlow

Parker Publishing, LLC
www.Parker-Publishing.com

Parker Publishing LLC

Lotus Blossom is an imprint of Parker Publishing LLC.
Copyright © 2008 by Jax Cassidy and Simone Harlow

Published by Parker Publishing LLC
12523 Limonite Avenue, Suite #440-438
Mira Loma, California 91752
www.parker-publishing.com

ISBN: 978-1-60043-034-3
First Edition
Manufactured in the United States of America

Cover Design by Jaxadora Design

Dedication

To Billy,

for your friendship, inspiration, and

being my muse during those dark times.

❤

Acknowledgments

I would like to thank my mother for her love and support, for being my rock during those rebellion stages, and for showing me that dreams do come true if you want it bad enough and are willing to work hard enough to get it.

To my sisters, Melissa, Jessalyn, and Kyme, for believing in me and making sure that there's plenty of ideas and drama to add to my stories. Thank you for always being there for me during those adolescent years and now as an adult.

To my nieces, Brianna and Chandler. You may be too young to read my books but thank you for your unconditional love. I'm proud of you both!

Thank you my "Fabulous Five", Kristen Painter, Eden Bradley, Eva Gale, Gemma Halliday and Lillian Feisty for being there for me during those rollercoaster days before and after I made publication history. I truly appreciate your friendship and love! Thanks for spending those endless hours on the phone with me, and for always being willing and ready to offer brilliant advice when I needed it most. You gals ROCK!

To Mark for always believing in me. Thank you for sharing a bit of culture and culinary expertise, for those endless hours of talking about life over several bottles of wine and a great meal, and for enriching my life.

To Jesse, my partner in crime, for being my sports and beer buddy. Most of all, thanks for all the laughs. My success is your success.

To Denita, a wonderful friend and supervisor, your support and kind heart has made it possible for me to get SIREN'S SEDUCTION written. Thank you for listening, advising, and giving me a reason to come to work every day. You are the best!

To my Lulu Crew: Dana, Ellenie, Robin P., Robin B., Kate Willoughby, and D'Anne Avner for spending those long hours on end with me at the café.

And last but not least, thank you Miriam and Jackie for your confidence in me, for allowing me to be part of your family, and for your kindness and understanding.

The Lotus Blossom Chronicles:

Siren's Seduction
By
Jax Cassidy

Cranberry Crumbled Cookies

Chapter One

The siren lured him with a melodic song of heartache and pain; painting such vivid imagery Niko Chow couldn't seem to push the tragic tale from his mind. He closed his eyes, soaking in the powerful, smoky voice filled with so much passion and conviction.

Donovan Matthews.

This stranger, this beautiful woman, was the reason he scoured every jazz club and trashy dive from Mexico to Los Angeles. The same woman he had overheard regulars affectionately nicknamed "Dove."

All for a bloody promise.

Niko blew out a frustrated breath, opening his eyes with a slow ease. He re-adjusted to the dilapidated surroundings of dim, fluorescent, red lighting that hid some of the imperfections of the cramped lounge. Dusty shelves lined the outdated purple and red art deco décor complete with scuffed floors, mismatched furniture, and worn out bar stools and booths. The place was a real dump of the lowest caliber.

Niko wasn't sure what possessed Dove to work at this shit hole anyway. He glanced over at the stage and the sultry voice pulled him back in like a wind tunnel, making it hard to resist visually drinking in his fill of those lush curves, big chocolate eyes, golden brown skin and silky raven's curls.

Simply mesmerizing. Those were the words that came to mind when he stared at the shapely physique and seductive performance.

Dove.

The name fit the woman, yet the Ella Fitzgerald voice mingled with the Billie Holiday sex appeal had been an unexpected charm. His lips twitched in humor, a smile never completely forming. She was definitely not what he had imagined.

While playing detective, all he had to go by was a battered ten-year-old photograph. By the looks of it, the beauty on stage was no way the same wide-eyed, pigtailed girl from the photo he carried in his wallet.

Niko grabbed the glass of scotch and brought it up to his lips. He paused, frowning at the habit he had not been able to kick. The sharp peaty aroma hit his nostrils, yet he inhaled deeply of the amber liquid

5

as if it would quench his thirst. With a mournful gaze, he placed it back on the table.

How long had it been now?

Niko hadn't stepped foot in a bar in eighteen months. Hadn't touched a drop in what seemed like an eternity. The powerful urge often assaulted him, coaxing him to drown his troubles, his own demons. But what would that accomplish? Another stint at rehab and some more lost time he would have to make up later?

The image of Gabriella Matthews appeared like an apparition in his thoughts. A quiet beauty with swanlike grace, mocha skin, big brown eyes and an infectious smile. No, Gabe wouldn't approve if he gave in. He damn well wasn't going to fall off the wagon now. Not even for a triad of naked whores drenched in scotch.

Niko's eyes returned to Dove, his eyebrows drew together, his lips stretched tight. Not even for the vixen squeezed into the skintight red 'fuck-me' number.

The torch song ended in a prolonged note, stirring something unfamiliar from deep inside. He shifted uncomfortably and rubbed his sweaty hands on his slacks. Had that feeling existed before? Niko zeroed in on her plump, scarlet lips and his cock jerked to life.

Hell, Niko didn't need the scotch to feel the intoxication of the chanteuse. She proved more dangerous than the booze. Everything about her screamed addiction waiting to happen and he wasn't ready to go there for two very valid reasons.

Feeling light-headed, Niko's sudden need for air seemed appropriate at the moment. He stood up abruptly and pulled several bills from his inside jacket pocket, throwing it on the table.

His eyes drifted back to Dove for a quick glance before retiring for the night. This had been the routine the past three days. Watch but don't speak. Don't maintain eye contact.

Niko wasn't a coward. No, he just couldn't bring himself to deliver the tragic news. He wasn't good at consoling anyone, let alone a stranger.

Christ, what did he know about relating to people? He had always been a loner. In fact, he could count the number of friends he had on one hand and still have some fingers left over.

You're growing soft, Niko. Get the hell out while you can.

Niko should trust his conscience more often. He turned to leave only to be met with a disappointed glare from the ever-flamboyant Saban Liu. The petite Chinese man stood firmly planted in front of him. His intimidation tactics never worked on Niko, especially dressed in designer women's attire.

Out of respect for their fifteen-year friendship Niko would not physically remove Saban from his path, although he certainly entertained the thought. He had to admit Saban made for an attractive member of the female persuasion. The man could carry off a sequined gown and designer shoes better than some of the society women he had known.

Saban had spent most of his life performing in drag and his reputation as a personal costumer had earned him an abundance of work with the elite entertainers.

With Saban's signature dramatics, the man threw his perfectly manicured hands on his hips in confrontation mode. "I'm ashamed to say your lack of initiative is unflattering. I thought you were much sexier when you were the brooding, take-charge type. I'm not liking the runaway bandit bit."

"Not tonight, Saban."

Saban scoffed, eyes flashing. "When will you be in the mood? For Heaven's sake, you've been searching for her for months and now that you've found Dove you need to tell her the truth."

"I'm leaving." Niko pushed past him only to be face head on by the one person he had intended to avoid.

"So soon?" The smoky voice injected.

Saban whirled around, squealing in delight, "Dove! So glad you've decided to join the party. Let me introduce you to my friend." He stepped aside and chirped, hands flailing in introduction. "Niko, Dove. Dove, Niko."

Niko felt uncomfortable. He hadn't expected to meet her so soon and something like a grunt escaped his lips in acknowledgement.

"My, aren't we friendly." Dove gave him a sarcastic smile.

"I was just leaving." Niko growled.

"Not yet, handsome." She placed a hand on his forearm.

"Saban tells me you're buying me a drink. Seeing as you've been ogling me during every performance, I think it's the least you can do. Besides, you wouldn't disappoint a girl would you?"

Dove couldn't believe she was talking to the stranger, let alone forcing her company on him. If Saban hadn't mentioned he knew Niko she never would have had the nerve to speak to him.

How could she not find the man attractive? Niko was fresh blood in this joint. She had seen newbies come and go, but had easily picked him out of the crowd on that first night. Who could miss the full on badass black ensemble and attitude to match? A Chow Yun Fat fantasy come to life.

Gorgeous was an understatement. Niko possessed chiseled features, a strong determined jaw, and a body that could only be maintained by a strict workout regimen. He wasn't bulky but lean in all the areas that counted most. His dark almond eyes and warm complexion against spiky charcoal hair revealed an even more exotic appeal up close.

Saban had called him Niko and the name appeared to be as interesting as the man. However, he apparently lacked social skills, but she could easily gawk at him all day without him saying a word. In fact, that seemed to be the routine from the beginning.

There was something to be said about dark and brooding strangers, they were a kind of trouble she didn't need. Yet, she couldn't help wanting to satiate the curiosity. Even now.

Niko motioned his head for her to take the seat across from him. His reserved nature should have put her off but there was a dark magnetism surrounding him that hooked her.

"Your weapon of choice?" He asked without any signs of friendliness.

She sat down, crossing her legs in a comfortable position before addressing him.

"Well, I'm sure you're a man who can appreciate a girl with distinct tastes." Dove flashed him her most innocent smile. "Ardbeg Ten. Straight up."

Niko raised a brow in interest and her heart sped up a notch. She imagined they had just made progress.

Saban who had been standing in observation grinned from ear to ear in obvious approval. "Let me do the honors. I've got some last minute things to take care of, anyways. Why don't you two cozy up… and talk." He gave Niko a knowing look then hastily sashayed out of the picture.

If Dove didn't know better, she would have assumed Saban was trying to play cupid again.

She placed her elbows on the table and clasped her hands together, leaning in toward him in an almost intimate gesture.

"Let me guess. You're just passing through. Being a friend of Saban's, he's coerced you into coming here to get you out of the stuffy hotel. You've only frequented this place because you don't have a desire to expand outside of the parameters of hotel and lobby dining. Am I correct?"

He paused for a long second and when he spoke she wasn't prepared for his directness. "Tell me, Dove. Why are you here? Your talents are wasted in this…place."

She pulled back and crossed her arms. "You get straight to the point, don't ya? Well, I really think it's none of your business."

"Really?" Niko's lips twitched. "But it is your business to make assumptions about me?"

A server briefly interrupted their discussion by setting the glass down in front of her. Dove eyed the generous portion of scotch. The drink would certainly knock her socks off. In truth, she wasn't much of a drinker but this man made her feel like she should keep her guard up.

Dove wanted to change the subject. She was never good at small talk, especially about herself.

She picked up the scotch as if she had done this motion a hundred times. "Will you join me in a toast?"

Niko's intense stare made her hands tremble and she hoped he hadn't noticed her reaction.

"Unfortunately, I've made a vow not to drink…" He let the sentence hang. His emotionless expression didn't hide the solemn tone.

A man with many secrets. He piqued her interest and Dove didn't know how to assess his behavior. Niko frequented bars and yet he had no desire for a taste. Strange, but fascinating. What or who could have made him take such a vow?

"A shame." She raised the glass. "I can respect keeping vows," she added before taking a healthy swallow.

The liquid burned a path down her throat, constricting her breathing in the process. Her eyes threatened to water yet she maintained her composure without so much as a flinch from the effects of the strong alcohol. No way would she give him the satisfaction of seeing her make a fool of herself.

The knowing expression on Niko's face made her come real close to disliking him.

He's not going to get to me. She swallowed hard to prevent the need to gag from the harsh contents.

"I admire a woman who can appreciate a good scotch." His voice held a hint of laughter.

Dove placed the untouched portion of the lethal drink on the table. When she could speak without her voice sounding scratchy she stated, "Looks could be deceiving."

"It certainly could." He gave her a lopsided smile that made her heart stop.

For a brief moment they were in their own subspace. She watched him through her lashes, her body blushing from his hard stare. His eyes sucked her in and made it hard for her to turn from the sexual energy between them.

A chill assaulted her and their moment dissipated all too soon. Even before Harry's hand touched her shoulder Dove knew he didn't like what he was seeing. She looked up and stared into the cold, steel blue eyes of her manager.

Harry gave her a disapproving frown. "Are you ready?"

"I'm catching up with an old friend." She snapped, jutting her chin out in defiance.

"Perhaps you've forgotten we have plans tonight," his tone clipped as if that was the end of the discussion.

Dove could tell by his expression that Harry wasn't in the mood to argue or put up with her resistance. A part of her wanted to tell him to leave her alone but she knew it was a dangerous line to cross. She had paid the price before and she didn't want to test him tonight.

Like an obedient child, Dove slid out of the chair without saying a word. She vowed to herself in that moment she would walk away when the time was right. She had to.

She smiled at Niko, feeling an odd sadness tug at her heart at being cheated out of time with him. "It was good seeing you again."

Niko rose up in gentlemanly fashion and nodded in acknowledgement. "I hope we will meet again under different circumstances." He raised a brow at Harry in annoyance at the intrusion.

"I don't believe it would be welcomed." Harry reached out and pulled Dove roughly beside him like a possession.

"Perhaps you should ask Dove what she would welcome." Niko's hard edge and poker face made him appear suddenly dangerous.

Harry tightened his grip on her waist and she flinched in reaction. Dove hoped Niko would discontinue the challenge before things got out of hand and she wasn't ready to be witness to it. These days she grew tired of Harry's anger and jealousy.

"Dove, my love, is it true you would welcome his company?" Harry waited expectantly for the answer she knew he wanted to hear.

She looked Niko in the eyes and for a brief minute she thought she witnessed a flicker of concern. Her pause made Harry's body tense up.

Niko's lips curved into a smile. "I believe the answer is in her lack of response." He raised his hand out for Dove to take.

Harry shoved her roughly behind him to confront Niko. "You dare come into my place and disrespect me? You're treading on dangerous territory."

She watched Niko's jaw tighten at Harry's rough treatment

"I suggest you curb your tone."

"Are you threatening me?" Harry sneered.

Dove reached for Harry's arm. "Let's go Harry. We don't want to be late." She tugged at him to follow, but he threw his arm out of her grasp.

Harry glared at her in resentment. "Are you trying to protect him, Dove? Is there something I should know about?"

"No. There's nothing going on. Please, let's just go." Her voice came out shakier than she intended. She placed her hand on his chest and gave him her most seductive smile.

Harry grabbed her hand and squeezed it painfully. "I've never known you to try so hard to get me to leave." He gave her a cruel smile before dropping her hand.

Niko spoke with a deadly calm. "A woman should be treated with respect, not as a property to be discarded without a thought when it suits you." His words made her stomach tighten with a newfound respect.

Chivalry was not dead after all.

Without warning, Harry seized Dove's wrist and shoved her at Niko.

Harry spat, "If the little whore wants to protect you, I would imagine your acquaintance is more that just friendly."

Dove could tell Harry's action snapped something inside of Niko. His calm demeanor was replaced by a dark cloud of anger. Without warning, he threw a punch that sent Harry sprawling on the floor. "I warned you about respecting women."

Within seconds the bouncers reacted to the situation, quickly advancing toward Niko. A loud scream from across the room startled her and momentarily distracted the bouncers.

Saban's hysterics were a diversion from the fight that ensued. Still shocked by Niko's reaction, Dove squealed when he swiftly scooped her up and threw her over his shoulder like a sack of rice.

"What are you doing? Let me down!" She commanded, panic setting in. Dove tried to kick her feet and used her fists to pound on his back in protest without much success. The death grip he held on her made it difficult to fight for freedom.

She felt helpless as Niko twisted left, then right to find the nearest escape route. The situation seemed to have escalated into total chaos.

Dove watched Harry stir from the floor, rubbing at his jaw as he tried to get up unsteadily. She hadn't expected Niko's punch to have so much power behind it and had been stunned by the action. A part of her was somewhat pleased that Harry would be on the receiving end of a punch.

When the bouncers lunged for him, Saban jumped in between to add further commotion. Dove wondered if the man was trying to help

Niko and she didn't know whether to be pissed off or grateful.

The bouncers looked at Saban as if they did not know how to handle him. This gave Niko ample opportunity to charge across the room. He sidestepped furniture and skillfully maneuvered his way around the panicked patrons in their haste to leave.

Niko pushed down the metal bar of the emergency exit and kicked the door closed behind him when they made it out. The shrill of the alarm was deafening as he took off down the alley with her firmly on his shoulder. He whipped around corners like a pro soccer player and headed straight for the parked car across the busy street.

He dropped her roughly on the seat of his convertible and hastily went around, jumping into the driver's side without bothering to use the door. Niko shoved the key in the ignition and fired up the engine. They took off so fast that all she caught was a glimpse of Harry and the bouncers running after them. The men slowly faded into tiny specks in the distance, into the darkness.

Dove's heart pounded hard against her chest. The fear seized her soul and she knew her life would never be the same again. The thought of reaching the point of no return filled her with a small kernel of hope.

Chapter Two

"Genius! Just great. I would imagine that when one plans a kidnapping, one should consider filling up the gas tank." Anger surged through her.

Dove tilted back her head for a better look at Niko and his unwavering seriousness. His toffee eyes held an impenetrable hardness and she wondered what had made Niko this way. She imagined he wasn't the kind of man to open up to anyone and that was a challenge she wanted to take.

As soon as she inhaled deeply to calm her nerves she knew she had made a grave mistake. The mixture of his intoxicating cologne and the close proximity made her long to lean in to smell his skin, savor his fragrance.

Embarrassed by her body's reaction, she needed to escape this heady need to give into her desires and run her tongue along the length of his neck.

The more aware she was of Niko the angrier she grew at the physical pull between them. Dammit, this shouldn't be happening.

His husky voice broke through her conflicted thoughts. "If you recall, I was leaving when you requested I buy you a drink."

Dove ignored his comment, pursing her lips at his statement. "Why couldn't you leave things alone? You *had* to be Mr. Chivalrous. You *had* to rescue me."

Niko gave her a look of irritation as he spoke, "Tell me Dove. How many more times would you have put up with his treatment before you walked away? Why do you let him disrespect you in such a way?"

"Don't you dare turn this around. You've just single handedly ruined me!" His question had struck a nerve and made her feel vulnerable, defensive.

Dove wanted to lash out and resorted to adolescent means by poking her finger into Niko's solid chest. "Who the hell do you think you are? To barge into my life, kidnap me, then act as if I had a hand in all of this." Her finger bounced right off with every poke, never sinking into his flesh.

The last action garnered a sharp pain that shot up her finger and her sadistic mind conjured images of a muscled chest and firm abdomen beneath the dark fabric. Her heart raced at the sudden desire consuming her. She entertained the idea of seeing him with his shirt off.

Her stomach fluttered with an unfulfilled longing that licked a path down her belly and settled between her thighs. It had been a long time since she'd felt this way. The slow burning and need to be held and made love to.

Niko took her off guard and grabbed her hand from further assault, jerking her roughly against him. He didn't give her a chance to respond as he captured her lips in one swift motion.

All thought flew from her head.

Warm. Soft. Hungry. Desperate.

She enjoyed his kiss way too much. He was not gentle, but his kiss meant to punish her for some reason. Dove's barrier slipped without resistance from the expertise of his mouth. When she sighed, he plunged his tongue between her lips and claimed her with a fierceness that left her breathless. Confused.

Losing all sense of rhyme or reason, Dove slipped her arms around his neck as she allowed herself to give into the heated kiss. His hands were gentle as they slid to her waist, pulling her even closer, holding onto her in such a way her knees grew weak. Pleasure soared within her.

Dove had never tasted a kiss so passionate before. Not even from previous lovers she had thought to be in love with. This feeling both excited and frightened her. She didn't know if she would ever trust her body again, especially when she was in this vulnerable state.

Niko explored her mouth with a thoroughness that made her mind scramble with uncertainty. What if he could see right through her? What if he knew she was a fake hiding beneath the designer clothes and attitude to conceal the scars of her past?

She had always been the fool. Donovan Matthews, an unfortunate runaway taken in by a man who wooed her with sweet words and broken promises. A man who transformed her into the woman she was now, not the woman she wanted to be. All for the need to be loved.

The erotic strokes of his tongue and gentle kisses made her body blaze with yearning. The man seemed to know exactly what a woman wanted by the way he paid attention to how she liked to be kissed and reciprocated the act.

This was the first time she had given herself over to the spontaneity of a kiss with a stranger. There was no doubt he knew what he could do to her.

Niko nipped at the corner of her mouth, running his tongue along her bottom lip. He continued his explorations with every kiss. His hands glided across her backless gown, lightly caressing her with the same gentleness until she shivered in his arms from the delicious effects.

Their tongues dueled and clashed, he teased her until her body screamed for more than just kisses. Her body craved to be touched. Craved to feel his naked flesh against hers. Reality struck her hard and fast at the realization that she was behaving wantonly. Her senses came barreling back to her and the shame stained her cheeks.

As if Niko sensed her hesitation, he pulled away and the sudden action left a chill between them. Dove's lips still burned from their fiery kisses. Niko's eyes were hooded and lust-filled when he looked at her. She realized he had a difficult time fighting whatever demons he possessed within him.

His eyes turned hard, yet she caught a brief glimpse of something else hidden in their depths. Something deeper.

The tension of the evening compounded with the intense attraction between them left Dove to react without thinking. Her chest tightened from the pressure and she had the need to get far away from Niko.

Without a word, she turned on her heels and took off without caring where she would go. Dove took a circular path around the car to distance herself, continuing her walk up the steep hill without looking back, without wanting to witness his rejection or ridicule for being too eager for his kiss.

Her heart felt heavy with humiliation and she felt like crying. She let out a bitter laugh. Dove had not shed a tear since her childhood and an ache spread from her stomach to her throat, until she could no longer repress the sorrow. The emptiness gaped open as the memories tumbled back into her mind.

What a fool she was! Her loneliness caused her to lower her guard and she had sworn to herself this would never happen. One touch from a man who showed the slightest bit of interest and she had come unhinged. God, she hated feeling this way.

How long had it been since she been held by a man, had been made love to? The lack of intimacy was starting to affect her. The hollowness in her soul grew with every move and she longed to turn back time. She never wanted anything to do with Niko!

Anger sparked within her and she blamed Niko's good looks, rigid seriousness, and dangerous appeal for playing havoc with her libido. Why did she allow herself to let him get to her?

Because I'm a fool! Her mind screamed.

Dove had always found attraction in the kind of men she knew would eventually hurt her. Discard her once they realized she wasn't good enough for them. Never wanting more from her than just a bedmate. Why did this happen to her? What did she do to deserve this treatment?

The pain became too much for her to bear. The wound grew wider with every thought and she hated this weakness. Dove touched her swollen lips, suddenly becoming infuriated by Niko's earlier forwardness. Angry he had kissed her without her consent, she cursed him for messing with her head, igniting her body with these indecent needs.

Damn him! He hadn't spoken a word since their getaway and now this. Why hadn't it stayed that way? Dove had given him the silent treatment with equal effort during their escape and if they had continued their non-communication, none of this would have happened!

In truth, she had rather not known what it was like to be kissed by Niko. Now she would never be able to erase the act from her mind.

Dove's lips tingled from the delicious memory, seething as she walked. Her thoughts kept returning to Niko and his enigmatic allure. Most women would be have been frightened by being whisked away against their will, but somehow she hadn't felt endangered by him. Never during that incident had she feared Niko.

How bizarre that she would feel safer in his company than if it had been some other stranger? It didn't seem right. Nothing seemed to be right since the moment she laid eyes on him. Why did he affect her this way?

Dove felt the connection with Niko but she didn't want to believe in such things. He was bad news and that may have been the draw, the reason. He somehow made her feel protected. As if nothing could ever touch her.

A cool breeze caressed the nape of her neck where bare skin was not covered by the lightweight material. She shivered, not from the cold, but from a deep sorrow digging into her soul. The only other person who had ever made her feel safe was her sister Gabriella. Someone she would never get a chance to know as adults.

How many years had it been since her family and home were ripped from her? She had given up on the possibility of ever being reunited with the one person who meant the world to her. The bitter tang of hurt lingered in her mouth. She had waited patiently, yet no one ever came for her.

Where were you Gabriella when I needed you?

The tears still did not come.

Dove had resigned herself to building the shell around her to recover from the abandonment and separation. She had blocked the pain by indulging in music, reveling in the beauty and emotions that could only be unleashed through her songs. Yet every time she sang, her heart broke all over again. Every note was unshed tears of loss and loneliness.

A frustrated sigh escaped her lips, her surroundings coming back into focus. Her lips curled unhappily from the reminder. Truthfully, the ride had amped her adrenaline levels and reminded her of those high school antics until their getaway had ended deep in the Hollywood Hills, then the car had run out of gas.

If this situation had happened to anyone else, she would have laughed at the absurdity. This, however, was a complete fluke that would never happen in a hundred years. Yet it happened to her! The gods were definitely enjoying the cruel joke.

Dove stopped to catch her breath. She glanced into the distance toward the Griffith Observatory; a brilliant Los Angeles landmark snuggled atop the Hollywood Hills in all its glory. Lights illuminated the place and a sense of warmth encompassed her.

She whirled around and caught sight of Niko leaning his hip against the car, his arms crossed patiently, as if he was expecting her to get the frustrations out. As if he knew she would return.

As if their kiss had meant nothing to him.

Even without saying a word she could almost read his thoughts. He had stirred things within her that didn't seem right.

Resentment ate at her insides at his audacity to take from her and act as if it was nothing at all. She marched back down the hill in her high heels and clingy dress without much grace to confront him. He got her into this mess and he damn well better get them out.

Dove stopped in front of him, crossing her arms, and eyebrows drawn together in stubbornness. "Well, Sherlock. What do you propose we do now?"

Niko straightened up from his leisurely position and from the angle of his stance he was a magnificent sight under the light of the moon. His dramatic features enhanced by the shadows and light, yet his eyes softened a fraction as he observed her in return.

His voice came out huskier than she remembered. "There's a gas station a few miles down. I trust you'd prefer to wait for me. If, when I return, you are no longer here I will understand your reason for leaving."

"Just like that?" Dove threw her arms in the air. "You kidnap me and now you're telling me to find my own ride. Do you know what a jackass you sound like right now? You owe me, buddy, and I'm not going anywhere!"

Dove watched his serious expression change. Did he just smile at her outburst? The transformation was so brief it could have been a figment of her imagination.

"As you wish. I would suggest you get in the car and put the top up and lock it."

"You are going to leave a defenseless woman alone in the middle of the night? Do you think that's wise?"

"What do you suggest I do? It would be quicker for me to go alone and get the gas than to have to worry if you'll be able to make it back to the car in those heels."

"Are you calling me a wuss?"

His eyes twinkled at her question. "Excuse me? It seems I can't say or do anything to appease you. I've decided that it's in your nature to be confrontational."

"How dare you. You don't even know me." Dove dropped her arms and she could feel the heat rise up her neck.

Niko laughed, a hearty, sexy laugh that took her by total surprise.

"What am I going to do with you? It seems that I have found someone equally as uptight as I am."

She resented his assessment of her. "I am not uptight! I am fun, which you wouldn't know the first thing about." She gave him a smug look.

He took a step toward her. "Really? You are telling me that I am not capable of fun?"

Awareness swept through her at his close distance. So close she could almost feel the heat of his skin. She shifted hugging her arms around her body for the warmth that would not come.

Dove lifted her chin, wanting to laugh at the ridiculous conversation they were having. "Yes, that's exactly what I'm saying."

Niko leaned in and his look turned mischievous. "Perhaps I do not believe you are the one capable of fun."

"Let's put it to the test then." She couldn't believe she was playing into his game. Dove was never good at running from any challenge, especially from a man who had shown zero personality up until now.

Her eyes darted around, trying to grasp any idea to prove her point. She was fun! How dare he assume she was incapable of this? The way he was staring at her suddenly made her feel self-conscious. What did he really see when he looked at her?

Niko watched the spark of fire in Dove's eyes and he had to admit she was like a wood nymph bathed in moonlight. A soft radiance surrounded her, caressing her form so delicately that his breath caught in his throat. God, she was stunning!

He could have well been on his way to the nearest gas station and back if not for Dove's ability to entice him with her sassy demeanor. He found something endearing about the way she bit down on her luscious

20

bottom lip, the expressiveness of her eyes whenever she spoke.

There was one thing Niko knew well and that was reading people. From his observations of Dove, he could tell she craved the adventure she had been deprived of for so long. Beneath the tough girl act she wore her heart on her sleeve. The vulnerable and sensual were a lethal combination and made her the kind of woman he should be careful not to allow too close.

Niko watched the scowl forming on her face and couldn't help noticing the loose strands of hair falling across her cheek. He wanted to touch the soft curls that framed her flawless latte skin. He didn't know what possessed him to reach out to finger a lone curl.

His eyes drifted to her mouth, so ripe and ready to be plucked. Dammit, but he wanted to taste her lips and see if that electricity would flow between them again.

Niko wanted to fist that thick mass of hair and make love to her against the car until she cried out her pleasures. He grew hard from the mental image and dropped the soft tendril as if it was a flame that burned him.

Always the one in control, Niko didn't like this impulsive side peeking out. Needing to avoid those damn sexy lips, he averted his gaze and looked off into the distance. A vision of a bright, majestic architecture sitting on the south-facing slope of Mount Hollywood loomed ahead and a plan sprang to life.

Was Dove all talk or a spitfire willing to prove him wrong?

"I've decided it is a beautiful night for a stroll. Would you care to visit the Griffith Observatory with me?" He walked passed her in the direction of the landmark without waiting for her to answer.

"You've got to be kidding. It's closed right now and security is probably tight up there." Dove let out a frustrated sigh before following close on his heels.

Niko stopped, turning to face her. "Are you afraid of breaking the rules?"

"I don't think breaking the law constitutes a fun evening." She pouted.

"Perhaps you aren't the risk taker I imagined you to be." He stuck his hands in his slack's pockets, turned back around and continued his ascent upward.

Niko grinned at how easy it was to provoke the little vixen. She was playing right into his hands. He didn't think a brief diversion before taking her home would harm anyone.

"I resent that statement. I'll have you know I was born breaking the rules! I'm a rule breaker." She puffed as she trailed after his quick footsteps, mumbling something inaudibly under her breath.

He could hear the clicking of her heels against the asphalt and imagined they weren't comfortable, yet he wasn't about to slow down for anything. He was out to teach her a lesson.

"Don't lag behind, unless you enjoyed being thrown over my shoulder. I haven't much patience for slowpokes."

"Not again."

"Are you sure about that?" He turned his head to give her a serious look. Dove hesitated and he noticed she had been ready to retort but thought better of it.

Good girl!

They made it to the top of the hill and Niko felt a tinge of guilt. The trek had been farther than he imagined and she looked like the shoes were killing her. He was compelled to tell her to take those bloody things off but he knew Dove would find an argument in any suggestion.

Niko stopped in front of the heavy chain links that secured the premises. The view of the observatory was spectacular and the sturdiness of the frame and the softness of the halo of lights surrounding it reminded him of present company.

He looked over at Dove who now stood beside him. The crisp night air and view of the city lights that stretched for miles on end seemed calming. Perhaps the effects created a comfortable silence between them as they soaked in the details. Niko noticed Dove trembling, yet she tried to put on a tough exterior.

Slipping out of his jacket, he draped it over her shoulders. She started to protest but allowed him to keep her warm. The woman was stubborn to the end, which was both annoying, yet an oddly adorable trait.

He straightened up and stared into those lucid chocolate eyes, eyes that held such innocence and hardships. Niko mustered a serious tone, "I think we ought to take advantage of being the only guests on the premises. Are you in?"

She wrinkled her nose at him as if she didn't know how to respond. When her response didn't come fast enough, Niko made up her mind for her. He swept her up in his arms and Dove squealed her protest.

Niko deposited her gently over the chains and onto the plush grass before jumping the barrier. Excitement rose deep in the pit of his stomach and the youthful exuberance filled his every pore.

Hell, he missed how it felt to not think, just act. Why hadn't he done something spontaneous every once in a while?

Responsibilities, that's why.

A sharp pain of loss seized him and he didn't want to think anymore. He decided to push his rational line of thought aside for one night. At this moment, he would rather spend what time he had getting to know Dove before it was lost. One stolen moment of pleasure to remember before it was all over with.

Niko wanted to honor his best friend's wishes and maybe work up the nerve to tell her the truth tonight. He had to do the right thing.

The time was now or never.

Chapter Three

He had a way of heating her up with a simple touch, a quick burn that wouldn't die. She watched Niko scout the grounds debating where they should start. Evidently the guards were not doing their jobs, as there was not a soul in sight to stop their impending activities.

The deserted location appeared as if the landmark was a playground only for them. This fantasyland conjured up an Alice In Wonderland adventure and she wouldn't be surprised if she witnessed a talking rabbit and the Mad Hatter popping in to meet them. The thought made her smile.

Stories were the only escape from the cold existence of a foster child. The grim reminder dampened her joy for a brief second but she had invested in the comfort of what those books had done for her. They had given her the freedom she never obtained.

Dove gazed at the perfection before her. How could such a place exist? The grounds were immaculate and the extraordinary structure embodied the vision of a place for people to discover the wonders of science. A place to delve into the planets and stars from within, and learn about the possibilities that lay outside the universe.

From what she had read, Dove couldn't believe tens of millions of visitors have walked the inside of the building, viewed the live planetarium shows, or simply came to gaze out towards the coast and the heavens. This was the cultural and scientific icon that had always fascinated her since she first visited as a teenager.

Not all memories had been bad. One foster couple had given her hope for a few short months, but like everything else, the happiness was fleeting. The gift that hadn't been taken from her was the advice to follow her stars to make a better life, a new existence in which she would finally control.

Her chest tightened from the heartbreaking recollection.

Those days were now gone.

Dove gazed at the Griffith Observatory, her hideaway when the world seemed to close in on her. When she felt lost and alone without any optimism. Many times Dove had looked to the skies for answers and she convinced herself Heaven was just an arms length away.

Those days, she believed that somehow, some way Gabe would see the signs and find her waiting in this safe haven. The notion was both absurd and childish. This was a valuable lesson she learned once adulthood caught up with her.

No use in reminiscing.

Dove grumbled, "I hope to God you're not planning on breaking in."

"I may look a fool, but believe it or not, I am no fool. We'd set off the alarms even before our shadows crossed the threshold." Niko rolled his eyes as if she was naïve in thinking.

"Okay, Confucius. I bet you didn't even have a game plan. What criminal act shall we attempt then?"

"Is there a possibility we may just enjoy the sights and view of the city without finding ourselves behind iron bars?"

Dove let out an exasperated sigh. "You're insufferable! You told me..." Niko placed a finger on her lips to quiet her and an urge to take the slender flesh into her mouth surprised her.

She stood frozen, afraid to move. The yearning for touch became overwhelming. She started to open her mouth and he shook his head, as if to tell her to keep quiet for a second longer.

"I'm sorry. I thought we had company." He dropped his hand, yet the damage was done. Arousal flowed through her. Her breasts grew heavy, her nipples hardened, poking through the transparent material even though she still had Niko's jacket securely around her.

Dove couldn't breathe. His closeness, his cologne, his look made her insane with wanting. She turned her head to catch herself from revealing too much. She caught sight of the public telescope and found a reason to escape his closeness.

"Since we're here. Let's look at this great city of mine."

Niko glanced in the direction of her line of vision and nodded. They walked silently to the edge of the railing along the overhang on the hills. She hadn't expected such a gorgeous night pregnant with stars and multi-colored flickers of light from the city.

The Hollywood sign glowed brilliantly not far from them and the quietness of the trees and shrubbery gave her a sense of peace. Dove hadn't expected him to stand so near, yet he had a way with invading her space. He leaned forward and closed his eyes.

She watched his face relax; all the muscles limp as if he connected to the earth. Could she connect with it too? Dove couldn't help staring. She wanted to run her fingers across the silkiness of his golden skin and feel her way across the perfect planes and angles of his face.

He slashed through the silence with a smooth, gentle tone, "Have you ever heard of such pleasures? Imagine the universe speaking and it sounds like a melody so sweet, so dramatic. I can see an orchestra surrounding me with their polished instruments and seasoned players, unraveling great tales of tragedy, yearning, love, loss. So haunting, yet so poignant."

Dove gaped at the image conjured in her mind's eye. Niko's use of language was so sensual, so erotic. His inflections on particular words made her panties moist with anticipation. If she had closed her eyes she would believe each word was a caress meant to stimulate her.

Niko's sharp intake and expelling of breath broke the magical spell. He straightened up and turned to lean his back against the thick iron railing.

"Tell me Dove, what brought you to the City of Angels?"

His simple question could have been easily answered if it was a passing conversation with strangers, yet between them, it seemed intimate, intrusive. She was a private person and wanted to keep it that way yet she didn't want to avoid the question.

Dove had avoided things her whole life and she decided to speak what was in her head.

"Foster parents." Dove said with a bitterness she hadn't intended. "My whole life revolved around my solid relationship with my sister. Of course, when children are too old to adopt for financial or other criteria, the younger of the two would be chosen. We were separated and I've never heard from her since."

The lump grew until it seemed lodged in her throat, difficult to rid. She cleared her throat, cocking her head to take a good look at Niko. Wanting to get any sign of a reaction from him but there was none, only an impenetrable blankness in his eyes. What was he thinking? Feeling?

He reached for her hand and pulled her to him. "I'm sorry," he said before wrapping his arms around her waist.

His action was so unpredictable that Dove's confusion compounded. She laid her head on his chest and felt his hand stroke her curls.

"You've had it hard. There's so much pain and loss out there, so much more..." his voice drifted off. "I've known loss so great I wondered if I could end it and nearly did."

She lifted her head and their eyes met. "Tell me about them."

Dove's voice sounded shaky, but this bizarre bond overshadowed the physical desires. She could honestly deem being held by him was a more intimate act than even the act of lovemaking.

"I don't want to speak of such things on a night like this. When those beautiful eyes of yours look at me that way," he confessed before his lips claimed hers.

The tenderness of his kiss was in contrast to their first. He brushed his lips softly against hers, nudging her to open for him, allowing his tongue to probe her. She moaned when his tongue flicked across hers. His gentle exploration delved further than just a mere kiss.

She shifted in place to lean her body fully against his. Dove captured his face with her hands, pulling him into her, wanting more than his gentleness. He responded by nipping at her bottom lips, suckling it delicately and she rubbed her body against him, feeling his stiff shaft against her stomach.

God, she was lost when he kissed her like that. How can such passion ignite between two people who have no history, no real knowledge of one another?

The heated kiss scaled to a new crescendo and she let her hands explore, feeling the solid chest and stomach muscles. She felt the perfect ripples of his abs and longed to lick them, trail her fingers around the shape. Her fingers glided up and down with gentleness and he seemed to welcome her curiosity.

Niko managed to capture her tongue, lightly suckling before he proceeded to satisfy her with the wonders of his lips. The man could kiss like nobody's business. She didn't care how much experience he had but if he continued along this path she would be putty in his hands.

"Hey, you two!" a loud voice boomed from across the grounds.

Startled, Dove pulled away, her heart pulsating so loud she thought Niko could hear it. She shook off the haze that had overtaken her and a giddy laugh escaped. She felt like they were teenagers being busted in a public place for PDA.

Her reaction garnered a chuckle from Niko. "Let's go," he blurted, taking her hand to flee.

They ran across the pavement, freshly mowed lawn, and their shoes resounding with a clip-clop whenever they hit the firm concrete. Their laughter rang in the air as the security guard chased after them. The heavyset man had no prayer catching up.

The run only increased her heightened roller coaster of emotions. She knew it would be a long time before she would ever experience a night like this again. Her bout of laughter grew until she became infectious and Niko had given into uncontrollable laughter with her.

When they reached the familiar iron links Niko helped her over and followed suit. The guard took her by surprise at his agility as he ran after them, closing in quickly. When he briefly stopped to call in for reinforcement it gave them the leverage to cover enough ground to separate them.

She was breathless and wheezing when they made it to the car. Niko yanked his door open and she slid across to the passenger side to allow him in. He pulled out his car keys from his pocket and by sheer miracle the engine roared to life.

They looked over at each other in amazement and laughed harder. Dove couldn't believe the car started and the speed of her heart rate increased its momentum.

Niko gave her a wide smile, "The filter must have been clogged when the sediment in the gas tank settled. Maybe we'll get a few more miles out of this baby before it stalls again. I think we can make it to the nearest gas station down the hill. What do you think?"

"Go. Go. Go!" she screamed. Turning her body as she peered up at the hill to make sure the guard wasn't visible. Blood pumped rapidly through her veins and the exhilarated state multiplied in intensity.

Dove felt like a rule breaker, a vandal running from the law, a criminal trying to escape authority even if their actions were purely innocent in nature. There was no doubt about it that the fire that had once been controlled within her was quickly blazing its way back into her soul.

They pulled into a gas station in a neighboring city and Niko filled the tank. He could see Dove fixing her disarrayed mass of hair and a smile crept up. This was the woman he imagined she would be. Carefree. Lovely.

He looked up to the Heavens and the moon winked back at him, beaming so bright and round as a saucer.

They say crazy shit happens during a full moon. His inner conscience teased.

The fact of the matter, Niko knew the hemisphere of the moon facing the earth was fully illuminated by the sun, making it appear round. The myths and stories were only conjured to make people believe in the magical elements. Werewolfs, strange acts blamed on such a phenomenon, these were all fictious wive's tales. He wasn't one to fall for it.

Yet, tonight in Dove's company, he would slightly bend to the powers of the moon. Only slightly.

Niko finished his task and slid in next to her.

She pulled off his jacket and neatly placed it on the seat between them before swiveling in her seat to address him. "Where to now?" Her reaction was like a child eager for more excitement, not wanting the night to end.

His lips twitched, not wanting the night to end for purely selfish reasons.

"I've an idea. Buckle your seatbelt and enjoy the ride." From the corner of his eye he could see the trademark pout, as if he had just crushed her fun.

Thirty-five minutes later they were seated across from each other in plastic chairs with two trays of hot dogs on the tabletop.

"Pink's! Such a classy joint. This is truly the highlight of my evening." She grinned at him before she picked up the mammoth hot dog and took a bite. The twinkle in her eyes confirmed her contentment at him choosing the place.

Granted this was one of the few venues open so late in the

evening but Niko thought it would be best to keep on the same line of adventure. Two big kids taking advantage of time.

Pink's was probably the most famous hot dog stand in Los Angeles. The place had started out as a large-wheeled pushcart. A mere hot dog wagon located on the rolling hills of weeds and open spaces during the days of the depression.

Over sixty-five years later, the place was a magnet attracting customers from all walks of life. A celebrity hang out and a club goers dream after a night of binge drinking. Located near the corner of Melrose and La Brea, crowds of people lined up regularly for a whiff of the aroma of fresh meaty chili and soft hot dog buns.

Not quite the place to take a woman like Dove to on a night out, but this was definitely an exception.

"Are you showing your snobbery? I've been wanting to come to this place for years and hadn't made it until now." He sunk his teeth into the hot dog and an explosion of ingredients overloaded his taste buds. "Wow. This was worth the wait."

Dove laughed as she took a swig of her Crush Orange soda straight from the bottle.

"I have always loved this little place. It's a throwback from the past and doesn't try to exceed anyone's expectation. It's what it is without trying too hard. I like that all levels of patrons have visited this spot."

"Whatever you say," he winked and polished off his first hot dog before moving onto the next one.

Dove wiped her mouth, then her hands with the flimsy napkin. She didn't look up when she asked, "Why are you here, Niko?"

He nearly choked, grabbing his drink and washing down the impediment by draining its contents. Niko placed the empty bottle down and straightened in his chair. He didn't think this was the appropriate time to disclose the truth, but perhaps he could answer her without going into details.

"I'm on a mission."

"What kind?" Dove bit her lip while she waited for him to speak.

His heart squeezed. "I made a promise to a friend I would deliver some news. The opportunity has never been available for me to do this."

30

She placed her hands on her lap and watched him silently. "Sounds serious."

"It is. One of the hardest things to do and I'm hoping that when I deliver it, I won't be faulted for Fate's hand in it. I am but a messenger." He hadn't meant for it to come out so curt. Bitter for being the one to do this.

He had assumed she would continue her line of questioning until he could finally tell her the truth, but she took him for a loop when she changed the conversation at hand.

"When we were at the observatory you told me you've known loss. Can you tell me now what you have lost?"

Niko didn't find relief in either topic. *Now is not the time, old man.*

"I'm sorry. I didn't mean to pry." She resumed eating quietly.

He pushed the tray aside and looked right at her. The way her eyes widened with interest, the way the light bounced off the lamppost and outlined every curve of her face, neck, breasts made his body hum in response.

She had to be a siren seducing him with her exotic powers. His eyes swept over those lips and he wanted to confess. Wanted to spill his guts to this woman who had mesmerized him in a short span of time. As if he had known her his whole life and the idea of such nonsense left an ache that scared the shit out of him.

"We had been together since college. She was so beautiful sitting under the tree studying for finals. She was the only woman who knew everything about me and still remained in my life. Accepting me for who I was."

He started up slowly and the memories poured in and added to the anguish. "We barely had time together. I worked too much. Slept too little. I thought I had done everything in my power to keep her happy and safe. In my eyes, I had perfection in my reach."

Dove pushed her own tray aside and her eyes locked onto his face, focusing on his every word.

Niko drowned in those caramel depths. A man possessed, he leaned in and cupped her face. "We were going to have a child," he choked up. "We were going to round off the fairytale..."

He could see her eyes tearing up and the damn erupted. The pain

31

gushed and the fear seized him.

"What happened, Niko? What happened?" Her voice was barely more than a whisper.

"I lost them both." He dropped his hand, suddenly angry with himself all over again. "I lost them because I had worked too much and wasn't there for her. Wasn't there to protect her."

How could she ease his pain? Dove watched him fight for composure. She could feel the hollowness, could relate to the loss as if it was her own grief.

The sorrow unleashed something buried inside of her and all she could think about was their naked flesh, feeling him deep inside her. That empty gap had grown into a sinkhole of longing. His ache became hers and a sensation of lust and animalistic cravings seized her body.

Dove needed oxygen. The air seemed dense, polluted by a fusion of thoughts and she panicked. She needed to go home. Back to her garden and the security it held within those walls. Her house was her only salvation away from such emotions.

"Please take me home. Niko, I need to go home."

She could tell her words had slapped him back to the present. The quick way he responded to her request lessened her anxiety and she was grateful.

Somehow the anxiety was the least of her uncertainties. She couldn't put her finger on it, but an eerie awareness washed over her. Pulling her under. Down, down, down until the grief sealed every particle within her.

Niko.

The voice whispered.

Niko.

Could he be her salvation? The buoy that would help her float to the surface.

Chapter Four

Niko walked her to the steps of the rich burgundy door. The color clearly enhanced by the blend of brick walls with ornate, cream trims and white columns.

This was her first purchase three years ago. She had scrounged every penny for a down payment on this home. Toluca Lake was an exotic hideaway tucked between Burbank and Studio City. Her place was hidden in a cozy nook untouched by the blaring noise of the city and the endless throngs of pedestrians.

A short fifteen-minute drive into Hollywood, yet it was a heavenly spot. She had dreamed of living in the quaint neighborhood since passing through years ago on a quick excursion. This was an area that conjured up the wholesome family life with the perfect children and perfect lawn. It was her very own paradise and she made damn sure she would own a piece of it one day.

Heat radiated off him and Dove pivoted around to face the man who had single-handedly turned her complicated world into an official disaster zone. They had not spoken during the drive and she welcomed the silence.

There had been an influx of thoughts that wouldn't quit, and making her shake uncontrollably from the abundance of the sensations. At one point Niko had draped the jacket around her without her realizing it.

Everything seemed a blur up until this point. Here, she stood gazing into the face of a person she had known nothing about and now felt as if she had spent a lifetime in his company.

"You're home safe." Niko's sentence was like a caress.

His face suddenly appeared tired, as if he had been drained by the burden on his weary shoulders. He gave her a forlorn smile that resonated through her.

"Perhaps, someday..."

"Please stay with me," she cut him off, laying a hand on his forearm. "I need some company for a short while."

He nodded and his expression still masked his thoughts.

Dove unlocked the door and they entered the lobby. She heard the soft click behind her and made her way through the living room. She placed her hand on the back of the sofa for support as she plucked the heels off one at a time. When her feet touched the cool, hardwood floors she felt an instant relief. Some of the tension dissipated and a happy sigh escaped her lips.

Niko watched her flex her toes and she grinned when she caught him watching her.

"Would you care for a tour?" She asked politely.

He was tempted to tell her he would enjoy stripping her bare and turning her over and across the sofa. The light from outside spilled through the oversized windows and cast a radiant glow around her form. The dress clung tightly around her and he could see the outline of her thighs and legs silhouetted through the fabric.

He could only describe her as a subtle, yet amorous siren. A poem to be written, a ballad to be sung beneath the stars. Niko couldn't say in words the portrait she invoked by just existing. Just being.

Had he ever experienced these sentiments for his own wife?

No. His psyche responded.

No. You have yet to understand.

Even though he did not want to consider this truth, he knew the answers without listening to his head.

"Yes, I would love that." His eyes were glued to her face. The exquisite details of her features were accentuated by the shadows and lights.

Dove bewitched him and her siren's song called to him. If he were a pirate sailing on the high seas, he would plunge into the icy waters to swim to her. Even to his death.

"First, let's have a drink," she coaxed, making her way to the kitchen to uncork a bottle of wine.

His ears did not hear, yet his eyes drank in every move she made. Niko was no stranger to music. He had been witness to sounds since the womb. His father was an accomplished musician. He, however, had never met his family's expectations. Could never compare to his siblings.

Oh, Niko had the gift. He hid it well for he had seen his father's obsession with bullying his siblings into a career they loathed. His sister had ended her brief life when the pressures had exhausted her, leaving her a lifeless shell at the tender age of sixteen.

When he was old enough to make up his mind he had fled. Became a man at eighteen, yet his love for music never waned. He had rummaged through the garage sales and found old jazz albums. On one occasion he had purchased an original LP of the great Ella Fitzgerald.

The good fortune became a consummate curse. His collection had grown out of control and he concealed these rare LPs in a private library in his home. A home that now sat empty for long stretches of time while he had committed himself in rehab, when he had tried to drown out his life after his family was stolen from him.

"Niko. Chow. Would you care for a glass?" She asked several times before it sunk in.

"I'm sorry..." he shook his head.

"The vow. Of course." Dove put back the glass and picked up hers for a sip of the red wine. She started to leave and stopped. She scooped up the bottle. "For the road." She winked and he couldn't help but give her a half-smile.

"Now, let's go." She walked over and took his hand, leading him through the living room, bypassing the hallway that possibly led to the bedrooms.

He was but a lost puppy following her lead. They reached the back of the house and he realized it led to a quaint garden. Niko turned the iron handle and opened into the most exquisite space.

Bamboo trees were planted in precise angles along a pebbled path. Wide, smooth patches of stone were firmly embedded in its center for a barefooted person to walk across without nuisance. He was amazed at how Zen-like and balanced the garden was. The tightly woven, yet sturdy bamboo fence was positioned a few inches higher than the house for privacy.

Dove looked to be on her third glass of wine even before they reached the back of the garden. An iron swing with vines wrapped around the top of the post gave it a fantasy appearance that added to the mystical elements of the area.

The calming sounds of water flowing freely and without hesitation caught his attention. He looked over to see a modest fountain tucked in the corner, water flowing from the rocks into a curved pool enclosed by tiles that looked to be hand-painted flying dragons along the trim of each piece. They flowed as freely as the water.

Niko's stomach constricted when he noticed the fresh lotus flowers of pale white and pink skimming the surface of the pool. A symbolic reminder and totally unexpected from this woman. He could tell she had a love for the Eastern culture and it warmed him.

The signs were starting to add up and he wasn't sure if Gabe was the culprit. He wanted to laugh. Her spirit would play these tricks on him. She was the kind of woman who pulled all the stops if she wanted to get her point across.

Just like Dove.

He dipped his hand in the water and scooped up a tiny bud.

"I'm going to grab another," she announced from behind him.

He twisted his head to look at her. She made quite a picture with those innocent eyes locked on him.

"Would you care for anything while I'm in the kitchen?" Dove swung the empty bottle as she spoke.

From his assessment, she looked to be a little tipsy.

"I'm fine." He turned back to the water and gently placed the flower back, watching it float on its own accord atop the whirling liquid.

He took a deep breath and decided he would tell Dove the truth. It was time to end this game because it weighed heavily on his conscience. Niko mentally prepared himself for the upcoming floodgates of emotions to come from this woman. His mission.

He sucked in a lungful of air, prepared to lay it all out on the table. He turned toward the door and closed his eyes for a few seconds of clarity. When he opened them again he watched her sultry figure make her way toward him.

Her hips swung sensually, her taut breasts pressed snugly against the material whenever it stretched from her every step. Again, the siren's song filled his head and clouded all rationality.

Dove stopped a few inches from him and set the bottle of wine on the edge of the fountain. She looked into the water, her eyes gazing over the lotus flowers. He watched her raise the glass to her plump lips and drained the remainder of the wine before licking her lips.

He longed to be her tongue, flicking across the silky surface. Hell, he longed for a few things that would be perceived as x-rated.

She set the glass down next to the bottle with an unhurried ease. Niko wondered what could be running through that beautiful head of hers.

Dove twisted around to meet his gaze.

"Do you know why I am drawn to the lotus? It symbolizes the four elements: earth, air, fire, and water. It's a spiritual emergence of a higher world directly from our physical manifestation."

Dove hooked her fingers beneath the spaghetti straps of her dress, pushing them off her shoulders with slow deliberateness. The material slid easily off her body as if her skin was made of satin. She stood completely naked before him, her caramel skin glistening beneath the dim light of the moon. Without hesitation, she took a step closer to Niko. So close he could smell her intoxicating perfume, easily touch her, and possess her.

Her smooth, smoky voice sliced through his indecent thoughts. "However, in Buddhist philosophy the lotus emerges from slime and corruption, then develops through the purifying water to emerge into the sunlight. They are seen as metaphors for the development of the individual being towards enlightenment." Her lips curved into a seductive smile. "Are you ready to be enlightened, Mr. Chow?"

What the hell was she thinking? Dove appeared calm on the outside, but inside she was a train wreck. Her head swam with wild dreams conjured up by too much alcohol. The temperature soared out of control when she saw Niko devouring her with his eyes.

The simple sweep of his lashes as he blatantly appraised her body had awakened the sleeping dragon inside. Each part of her skin heated wherever his eyes skimmed and lingered. Oh, he wanted her. A woman could not misconstrue that look. The one language two people spoke without saying a word. It was all in the eyes.

Dove cozied up next to him, slipping her arms around his neck and stood on tiptoes to draw him in for a kiss. His resistance melted as soon as their lips connected. One second he appeared unresponsive, the next he latched on to her with a fervor so impassioned she had a hard time catching up.

Damn, but the man could kiss!

His hands glided across her back, gently roaming to her shoulders, moving downward until he reached the edge of her bottom. He stopped and pulled her closer, his tongue flicking across the corners of her mouth before coming in for a deep kiss.

Niko's methods were skilled as he palmed her cheek to move her head just so, to enhance the thrill of the motions of his mouth and tongue. This was no simple kiss. This was out and out orgasmic without the consummation.

Dove had a handful of sexual encounters but Niko had an aura of expertise and tranquility about him that could easily entrance her. Magic hands. Soothing and healing as he ran them along every curve of her back and shoulders as if to memorize her.

Her fingers flew to his shirt, unbuttoning hastily until she reached the last one. She pushed the fabric off his shoulders and it bunched at his forearms. Her hands explored his chest and stomach with the same languid strokes he had caressed her with. Their lips never unlocked for more than a few seconds except to take in air.

Desperation, a ravenous need to be fulfilled inched its way down to her womb. She pulled away and unbuckled his belt, pushing it aside while she maneuvered his zipper. Dove dropped to her knees and when she unleashed his manhood from its confinement she gasped at her discovery.

His shaft hung solidly for her to inspect. Thick and rigid, simply beautiful with its elegant appearance. So smooth and ready to be taken fully into her mouth.

She closed her eyes when he touched her hair. This could only be considered as erotic. To her, erotic could be expressed as something greater than sex alone. When he ran his hand through her curls, across her skin, her body tingled and her senses were heightened from the motion. She indulged in the repetitive strokes and desire triumphed over her own pleasures.

She wrapped her hand around his cock, barely able to close around its width. Dove looked up at him and smiled at a thought. The myth was truly shattered tonight and she held the proof in her palms.

Niko looked down at her and he unleashed a moan when she

covered his rock-hard staff with her mouth. Dove wasn't afraid to taste every sweet inch of him if she could. Her mouth worked in rhythm with her hands as she sucked and licked him. Running her tongue across the head of his manhood before continuing the rhythmic movements.

He increased the pressure of his hand on her head, guiding her during her ministrations and she soon found ways to please him. She could hear the increased breathing; feel his reactions whenever he enjoyed something she did particularly well.

Dove discerned how powerful she was in this position. She was in control of his pleasures and relished in the ability to make him feel good. She wanted him to remember tonight because she knew tomorrow would be the last time she would ever see him. She would make sure of it.

This night was as much for her as it was for Niko. Even with the intoxicating effects of the wine, she had never been this uninhibited. She was both free and alive. Dove could be whatever she wanted to be without caring about the consequences.

She was consumed with the need to abandon the shield around her heart, to give him a glimpse into her world. This could be a grave mistake yet one she was willing to risk. She didn't want to dismiss the link between them. Deep down she truly believed this was meant to be.

Dove was meant to give herself over to him.

Just for one night.

Niko stopped her from taking him over the edge, she was certain he was close by his labored breaths. He reached down and pulled her up, placing a hand around the base of her neck to draw her forward. He kissed her roughly, then with delicate tenderness while her mind emptied of all thought.

She suddenly felt weightless, floating across the garden for some time until her body sunk into a fluffy cloud that molded to her flesh. Dove opened her eyes and the world spun around her. She let her head settle back into the softness and heard the swish of fabric on the floor.

Niko slid easily between her thighs and when his skin brushed up against hers, she wanted to weep from the contact. He stroked her hair and placed angel kisses on her forehead, cheek, and chin. They fit comfortably as if this was a natural occurrence.

Dove wiggled beneath him, trying to feel closer to him and he halted her movements by running his tongue from the spot behind her ears down to her collarbone. She shivered with delight until he captured her breast with his wet, hot mouth. He licked and suckled, squeezing her breast while savoring her.

She arched her back. Loving the firm grip, the slow caresses as he feasted on her. When she thought she would die if he didn't enter her, he slid down her body and pushed her thighs apart.

"Oh, God," she cried when he covered her mound with his mouth. He parted the folds, licking her, tasting her, exploring the recesses kept sacred from the world. She didn't recognize the sounds coming from her lips with every suckling, every flick of the tongue.

She felt as if he knew every inch of her.

The tension built gradually until he ran his thumb across the sensitive nub, then replaced it with his mouth. His teeth slid across and she jerked. The pressure grew, mounting, mounting until she clutched his shoulders. Digging her fingers into his flesh when he started to suck on the aching flesh, the core that held her path to ecstasy.

Her hips moved as he fucked her with his tongue the same way she had longed to be taken. His mouth wouldn't quit as he satiated her needs like crashing waves against the unyielding rocks. She couldn't fight the sensations any longer and soon gave into the rapture of climbing to great heights before plummeting down, lower and lower, out of control.

Dove bucked as she screamed out her pleasures. She felt like she was drifting across the universe, watching the planets rotate around her, tumbling into a sanctuary guarded by Niko. She could feel his heart beating hard against his chest when he moved up to cover her.

He wrapped his arms around her and rolled with her to his side. Holding her tight, so tight she couldn't breathe. Her body hadn't recovered form the mind-blowing orgasm yet she snuggled up to him and leaned her head against the crook of her neck.

Her eyes were heavy, so very heavy she could barely keep them open. The last image that flashed in her mind was of Niko. Their energies expanding, heat rising. Escalating until she finally gave into the possession and their spirits melded together to form a union of the souls.

Hearts beating as one.

Chapter Five

Dove rolled over, her arms outstretched, reaching for an empty bed. Her head throbbed as if someone had pounded it with a sledgehammer during her sleep. She gripped the sides of her skull and dropped back down against the pillow.

The images were fuzzy as they came in and out like a television set going haywire. When things began to make sense, connecting like pieces of a puzzle, she was hit by the reality of what happened last night.

Her stomach churned from uneasiness, threatening to push the contents up if she didn't calm down. She had thrown herself at him and he refused her. Why did she believe he would be different? That he could want her.

Dove closed her eyes, feeling the sting beneath her lids. Dammit, why couldn't she cry! At least then, she would finally feel human again. She needed this release so she didn't have to push every pain, every hurt into a dark hole until she became numb. Devoid of feeling, no longer alienating her true self from the world.

Stung by Niko leaving her without a word or a goodbye, she blamed her own stupidity for thinking he actually cared. She was a fool who longed to live a fairytale. Why hadn't she learned? She purposely built a wall around her to avoid something like this.

Never again.

Dove willed herself to go through the motions of showering, dressing, and heading out to face Harry. She would get through the day even if killed her.

I'm already dead inside.

She made it to the front door, her hand on the knob. An overpowering sense of sorrow swept through her and she dropped to her knees, hugging herself as the grief struck. The profound comprehension wracked her body at such a loss.

Gabriella had been everything she'd known since her parents died. Her sister had been her reason for believing. Why did this have to happen to her? Why did it hurt so much? Anger and hatred fueled her and she let out a deafening cry, unable to hold the pain any longer.

Why did they all leave her? How dare they walk into her life and turn their backs without a thought! Dove wanted to die, at least then she wouldn't be faced with a future of regret. A future in which she would no longer care if she wasted into nothing, left alone and bitter.

She had known loss. She had tasted heartache and it was as empty as the last ten years. If not for her music, she would have gladly ended it all. Hope had kept her alive. The hope that Gabriella would one day rescue her from years of desolation and loneliness. All she needed was the knowledge that she had a family.

Gabe had promised her she would take care of her.

"You lied to me!" Dove shouted to the room. "You lied and left me all alone. You didn't love me. You never did."

The tears never came and she wondered if this was a curse that would never be broken.

Her heart bled, trickling with every memory. Now Niko had abandoned her too. Did she mistake desperation for a connection? Had she grasped at any reason to feel loved? Be loved? She didn't know who she was anymore and the hollowness now included the rejection from the one man she believed would save her soul.

Harry watched her from the back corner table as she sang. This was a way for him to keep an eye on her and an invisible leash he controlled. Dove had been wary of his friendly demeanor, even though the chill of his tone could have easily formed icicles on the windows.

Had it been nearly a week since Niko left her?

Dove brushed off the thought before it became a full-fledge internal monologue. From her peripherals she could see Harry, the look of disgust clearly visible even as he sat in the darkened section.

The one thing she hated most was the silent treatment. It had been different with Niko, but with Harry it was a warning that he had something up his sleeve. She had been witness to his wicked handling of situations in the past and it was not a pretty scene.

The wound had not healed from her breakdown the first day she returned to work but she had put on the invisible mask and had started to work like the professional she was. Only one more song left for the evening and she was ready to wrap up and go.

Dove needed to get away. She wanted to go home and curl up into a ball in the safety of her private cocoon. She had learned to deal by enclosing herself and escaping into the darkness. No one could hurt her there. No one would be able to touch her in this sacred realm. Not even Harry.

The music started up and her eyes settled on the empty table that Niko once occupied. Tonight the patrons were sparse but she wasn't concerned. The business would still pour in with the amount of alcohol the regulars consumed.

Her eyes moved passed the table to scan the familiar faces. For a brief second she believed she conjured up an image of Niko in the darkness. His gaze warmed her belly and the first note filled the room.

This was a song she had written years ago, a story about yearning to find her soulmate. The one person who could finally gift her with safety and true love. *Could this ever happen to me?*

Dove stepped up to the microphone, placing her hand around the plastic clip and leaned in so close her lips almost touched the head of the mic.

Her voice came out husky, emotional as she sang, "I have traveled to far off places in search of you. I have sung a siren's song in hopes of seducing you. Seek me out, save my soul. Seek me out and make me whole." With every note she poured out the contents that weighed heavily in her heart. "I thought I could stand alone. I waited long enough for my mate of souls. In truth it was my heart you stole. So seek me out, make me whole. Seek me out, don't leave me in the cold."

As she sang, she found this a kind of therapy that relieved her anguish. This is why she was here. Music was a way for her to reach out to him. Reach out for understanding and pulling strength within herself to walk away.

Niko was the reason she had fought every day to deliver her best performance. He was the one she had waited on, and like the song, he made her feel safe. No matter what had happened, he had filled that void for a few hours, maybe a lifetime.

She didn't want the song to end. This was a way of reaching out to the man who haunted her. He had been in her dreams; he had kept her protected all those days Harry took out his anger on her. Niko had been the faceless man of her dreams that would one day show her the way back home.

Dove smiled as enlightenment sank in. She always had her dignity. Her voice had supplied Harry with the comforts that surrounded him and if she were to leave he could not stop her. She would no longer fear she could not stand alone. Her music would get her to the place she belonged. Maybe one day she would even have the ability to find Gabe. Find Niko.

She had closed her eyes for a brief moment and when she re-opened them the apparition disguised as Niko had vanished. He may be gone from her life but in her heart she would forever keep him locked inside.

Dove's last note soared, higher and higher, so high the room trembled from the power of her voice. She was in control. This was her swan song to this hellhole. Good riddance! If she never had to look at this place again it would be a blessing.

When the song ended, silence had stolen her audience's voices. Dove dropped her hands from the mic and stepped back as the eruption of claps and whistles brought her eyes back to the crowd. The place was packed. More so than it had ever been in years.

Her intense focus on the song had faded out the crowd. She had wanted her last song to be for one person. Dove had sung the siren's song for Niko, and Niko alone.

The weight lifted and excitement coursed through her. This feeling was the same spontaneous zaniness she had experienced with Niko a few nights ago. Dove didn't want the exhilaration to end. Especially when the night was just beginning!

In her rush to leave she had tripped on her descent down the stage stairs. Harry steadied her. When she lifted her head she saw the anger blazing in his cerulean eyes.

"You haven't sung that song in a while. Was it for your precious Niko?" He sneered into her face.

His handsome features now distorted into the ugliness that she had known him always to be.

"Yes, Harry. It was for Niko and it will never be for you," she spat back.

"Whore! I made you. I took you from the streets as the tramp you were and transformed you into this." He grabbed her arm with one hand and squeezed her chin with the other.

Dove winced. "You're hurting me."

Harry dropped his hands and straightened his jacket. "Go change and when we get back to my place you will please me. Just like old times." His voice commanded and the tone sent an icy chill through her.

She shook her head and all the pent up aggression of years of abuse surfaced. Dove balled her hands into fists and pounded on his chest with all her force. "I'll never succumb to you. Do you hear me! You bastard!" Her fingers unwound and she started to claw at him. Needed to inflict the same pain he had done to her since the first time he laid a hand on her.

Never would Harry treat her with disrespect again. She was no longer the girl who feared him but a woman who despised him.

"You bitch!" Harry wiped his bloodied face.

He raised his hand and struck her so hard she stumbled back.

If Dove had located a weapon, she would have surely pulled the trigger. Her rational brain told her to run. The damage was done and she needed to flee before he used her up and spit her out like the dozens of times before.

Her lips had split open from the impact of the hit and she tasted the saltiness of her own blood. She wiped her mouth with the back of her hand and laughed bitterly.

He will never touch me again!

"It must feel good to hit a woman with half your strength. Doesn't it?" Dove gave him a wide grin. "Do you think I would ever want you? A monster cloaked in designer suits without any chance of redemption..."

Harry had frozen in his place at her insult. She imagined it had registered in his head that he had abused her before the public, not behind closed doors.

She didn't wait to see what happened next. Dove whipped around, running straight for her dressing room. She grabbed her purse and any personal belongings, including a photograph of herself and Gabe as children.

Clutching her personal contents tight against her chest, she exited through the back door into the alleyway. She stopped for a quick breather so she could decide what course of action she should take.

The gambit of emotions ran amuck. Hurt. Anger. Confusion. All these things bombarded her at once and her eyes burned. Her lips ached and she craved the comfort of Niko's arms. She had broken the chains that bound her and it felt good despite the consequences.

A tear trickled down her face and Dove wiped it with her fingers. She raised her hand in the direction of the light. Some overhead building lamps illuminated the alley and the liquid glistened to reveal the proof.

The tears rolled. Fat unstoppable tears streamed down her face and she laughed at the miracle. Dove was not some freak after all. She was human!

Where are you Niko? I need you here with me.

The tears clouded her vision and the face that materialized belonged to Niko. She blinked, startled when the figure didn't evaporate like a hallucination.

"Dove." Niko called to her.

She wiped the tears for a better look and the items she had been holding slid out of her grasp.

Dove ran for him, jumping straight into his arms as he caught her, whirling her around in a circle. When they were at a standstill, Niko held her in a crushing hug. He raised his hands and clutched her cheeks, planting a smacking kiss on her lips.

"I thought you were a dream. I thought you had left." Dove touched his face, marveling at his striking features.

He touched his nose to hers and said, "It was more difficult to stay away. I needed to see you again."

Niko leaned in to kiss her and she let out an 'ouch'. He pulled back and took a good look.

"He hit you." His tone chilled her to the bone.

"It's okay. He'll never touch me again. I promise," she consoled yet the words fell to deaf ears.

Dove could feel him trembling with anger and that terrified her more than meeting Harry's wrath.

The sound of the steel door slamming shut made them both look over at the building.

Harry's neck was as red as his tie. "What do we have here?"

She noticed Niko had balled his hand into a fist at his side. This was definitely bad news.

Dove maneuvered between the two men and her lack of judgment made her an easy target. Harry stepped up and grabbed her hand, pulling him to him. "So the whore has managed to seduce you with her body. Tell me, Niko, does she pleasure you the same way she did with me? Did she ride you with enthusiasm so she could get what she wanted out of you?"

"You have crossed the line. You've just fucked with the wrong man." Niko took two long strides toward Harry.

Harry shoved her aside and swung with all his might at Niko who ducked with expertise.

Steadying himself, Harry pulled his fists up in a boxer's stance. Dove knew the man had years of training as a boxer and worried that Niko wouldn't be able to hold him off.

Harry threw another punch and Niko dodged it. After several rounds of missed strikes, Niko struck back, his fist landing soundly against Harry's ribcage.

Was that a crack she heard?

Niko bounced backward and whipped around to land a roundhouse kick at Harry's head. The man collapsed on the floor.

"Kickboxing champion," Niko bragged yet his voice belied no humor. His eyes had transformed into black slits as he looked down at Harry.

Niko commanded, "Get up. Get up and hit me you prick. See if I won't hit back."

Harry crawled to his knees and managed to get up on his feet. "I'm not afraid of you. Do you know that her mouth is not so clean? Did you know that Dove can do things with her mouth that would turn a saint to sinner," he laughed cruelly.

Dove cringed, knowing full well that Harry had turned an intimate occurrence when she thought she believed she loved him into something filthy. Dirty.

"Isn't it true, darling?" Harry continued his demented laughter.

The events that followed became a blur. Dove watched in horror as Niko lunged at Harry, knocking him to the ground. Swift punches connected in succession, and firmly hitting its mark every time. Harry's face became a bloody mess and after Dove had recovered enough to respond she ran over and covered Niko's fist.

"Stop. Stop. Please stop," she begged him from throwing another punch.

Harry croaked, "Y...yes. Stop. Don't kill me. I'll wash my hands of her, I swear it." His head rolled limply against the concrete.

Niko was panting. He had exhausted himself from using all his strength to seek revenge for her. She felt the emotions well up and a tear slid down her cheek. He had defended her and she was deliriously happy.

Whatever trance Niko was in, he snapped out of it when Dove followed him, her hand still covering his.

"It's over," she said and raised his battered fist to her lips.

Niko nodded and helped her gather her belongings. She never looked back at Harry to see if he stirred. Perhaps Niko had beaten him unconscious, which was well deserved. She didn't give a damn. He would never touch her again.

Harry was dead to her.

He had died in her eyes the day he beat her so bad she couldn't move, couldn't show herself in public until the wounds healed. This was payback and as gory as it was witnessing the fight, she couldn't help feeling like she had been the one doing the pummeling and not Niko.

Chapter Six

Dove was still in awe of the Italian Renaissance neoclassic hilltop mansion located on the Gold Coast. How could Niko afford this place? She was certain anyone who was able to own a piece of property of this caliber in San Francisco had to have serious dough.

She placed the last of her folded t-shirts into the drawer and shut it gingerly, scared to ding or scratch the expensive Italian handcrafted dresser. Stepping back, she scanned the guest bedroom and thought it was the size of her living room and kitchen put together.

Niko had some classy taste. It occurred to her that the environment fit the man. Everything about this house reflected his formal nature. Precise, organized, and somber.

She couldn't conceive of how his wife had dealt with living here, an empty shell when her husband worked long hours to give her this luxury. Dove sensed sorrow, isolation. She didn't know if she could wake up each night to a cold bed. Without the warmth of a lover.

She imagined he must have spent nights in his office while the woman slept alone. She shivered, hugging herself tight as goose pimples covered her bare arms. This place definitely was much too big for the likes of her. Dove lived a modest lifestyle and this seemed to be wasteful living. No matter how grand Niko's home was, she believed he only kept this place as a reminder.

When they arrived here, Dove had been apprehensive about entering because it appeared to be a cold and lonely place. Even with the expansive Golden Gate and Bay views from almost every room, she wondered what possessed someone to be so extravagant.

Niko hadn't given her a full tour due to the early morning hour of their arrival. They had driven five and a half hours and she was in for a rude awakening when it finally registered that he resided here.

This was indeed Silicone Valley. Lavish houses lined at a perfect distant side-by-side, each more magnificent as then the next until they pulled into the private winding drive of his hilltop mansion.

From what he had told her, the house contained a Grand reception hall, elegant formal rooms, and a graceful marble stair leading to the family level.

There were seven bedrooms and even more bathrooms, a library, music room, office, recreational room and an elevator. To top it off, there was a private tennis court and a garden that she was certain made hers look pale in comparison.

Dove recalled the period details throughout the home and knew Niko must have spent a fortune on the interior decorations. All of which were tasteful and elegant, not overdone.

Where was Niko? She wondered what he was doing at the moment. Perhaps sleeping. She frowned at the prospect of climbing into the huge bed in a foreign place uncomforting. Of course, she had been disappointed when he had taken her straight to the guest bedroom instead of offering to share his with her.

What did she expect? She didn't know if he was giving her mixed signals or being respectful of her privacy. She scoffed. It wasn't like they would just pick up where they left off that night they nearly made love.

Dove changed into a comfortable thigh length nightgown and tried to get shuteye. She rolled around and punched the feathered down pillow as if that would help cushion her head any better. Her mind kept wandering back to Niko and a barrage of questions filled her head, conjuring up thoughts of the mafia and shady dealings.

Where did he get his wealth from anyway?

The absurd notions swirled until she gave up on any chance of sleep. The ordeal of the evening had been too unsettling and she had a sudden craving for something warm. Maybe a warm cup of tea or milk. She kicked off the comforter and got up, hoping she would be able to find the kitchen.

Dove let out a laugh. "Maybe I'll be able to find my way back to my room without needing a map."

She wasn't usually a fraidy cat, but this place was massive and it gave her the spooks. She quickened her pace down the length of the hallway and hastily took the steps that led to the lower level. Dove recalled seeing the kitchen and hoped her memory wouldn't fail her now.

She was singing softly under her breath for a bit of confidence and stepped into the kitchen, coming to a dead halt.

"For fuck's sake!" she screamed, startled at seeing Niko seated at the kitchen island. She hadn't anticipated he would be awake too.

He dropped his spoon and the clank reverberated through the kitchen. "Christ! What are you doing up?" Niko exclaimed.

They both looked at each other and laughed heartily at the situation. She couldn't help being invigorated by the thought of freedom. Would she ever get used to not having to look behind her at every turn? Could she live this new life without fear or guilt?

Yes, she knew Niko would make sure of it.

Dove relaxed knowing Niko was not the kind of man who would terrorize her like Harry had done for years. With him, she felt tranquility and a sense of purpose to get back on her own two feet. She would take each day at a time and worry about her personal affairs once she settled here.

She walked over to the island and took a stool across from him. Niko appeared genuinely pleased to see her.

"Would you like a cup? I just made the Darjeeling tea." He didn't wait for an answer and stood up to grab another cup.

He poured the hot liquid into the porcelain cup and the steam rose, filling her nostrils with the familiar floral aroma. Her mouth watered at the eagerness for a sip to warm her up.

When this Indian tea was properly brewed it yielded a thin-bodied, light-colored liquor. From the look of it, Niko had it down to a science.

He held up the cream and she nodded for him to add a dollop in.

"Thank you for reading my mind." She smiled, stealing a glance at his face.

They sipped the hot liquid in silence and the flavor burst in her mouth. A tinge of astringent tannic characteristics with a musky spiciness hit her palate, then a sweet cooling aftertaste.

She closed her eyes and enjoyed the warmth spreading through her. The tea tasted like heaven and when she opened her eyes to look at him, she realized he was only wearing black silk pajama bottoms. His muscular upper body was exposed to her wandering eyes.

Niko was sumptuous and her eyes drank in the sensuality of his physique. Lean body, muscled arms, a solid chest and abs that belonged in a fitness magazine. She swallowed, her mouth watering from the urge to run her hands across his sculpted body.

This was the first she had seen him in the light since their last interaction, a hazy wine induced memory, yet her hands still remembered every detail.

His eyes lit up in amusement at her appraisal.

"I've always had trouble sleeping in new surroundings." Niko attempted small talk to break the awkwardness.

She nodded, her eyes froze on his lips, drawn by the perfect shape and all she could think about was kissing him.

"That's true." She blinked and looked away. Her cheeks felt hot.

She heard the scuffing sound of the stool move across marble floors and when she looked up he was next to her. Niko nudged her chin up with his knuckle. His eyes searched her face, reaching into her thoughts.

He bent his head and swooped in for a kiss that tasted as delicious as the tea. Warm, sweet, and tantalizing. Her heart hammered and she felt the blood coursing through her veins like an awakened river.

Niko was gentle, his kisses sent new spirals of ecstasy though her and when his tongue finally probed her mouth she needed more. Now was not the time to be gentle. She wanted to be satiated, consumed. His kiss turned urgent and he pulled her to her feet, dragging her body next to him.

He weaved his fingers through her hair, massaging her skull as he kissed her and she returned his kiss with reckless abandon. Niko pulled away and her protest died on her lips when he placed his mouth on the nape of her neck, kissing the pulsing hollow at the base of her throat in such a way her body hummed with delight.

His warm lips grazed her earlobe as he teased the sensitive flesh. This left Dove with a burning desire, an aching need, for another kiss. As if he read her thoughts, he moved his mouth over hers, devouring its softness with an intensity that left her panting.

He took what he wanted with his velvet tongue, her body eagerly responded and she wrapped her arms around his neck. Wanting to get closer, yearning to be pleasured in ways that a kiss could not fulfill.

Niko gripped her ass to lift her up and she wrapped her legs around his waist. He carried her across the kitchen and sat her on a counter against the wall. She gasped from the cold tile, her senses heightened by desire. He leaned her back against the wall and bunched up her night gown, parting her legs before he dipped between her thighs.

She let out a loud moan when he ripped her flimsy panties off with one hard yank and threw them on the floor. Dove felt the chill of the room and his hot mouth soon heated her up. His tongue explored the delicate folds before plunging into her with enthusiasm. She wanted to come on the spot.

His hands gripped her thighs as he feasted on her, sucking the tender flesh, teasing the hard bud until she scratched the tile, hoping to find support that wasn't available.

Her moans escalated and she squirmed, so ready to let go. She could hear his own moans against her and the vibrations only added to the tension. She reached out a hand and clutched his shoulder, lifting her pelvis up, grinding into his mouth as the first blissful wave hit.

Dove cried out as the release she yearned for barreled through her body, her chest heaving and her elbows threatening to buckle. Niko straightened up and tenderly wrapped her in his arms, holding her close to him. She could hear his heart pounding at the same speed as hers.

She turned her face to kiss his shoulder and he buried a hand in her hair, kissing the top of her head. Moments passed before he swept her up in his arms and carried her up the stairs to his bedroom. He laid her down across the plush bed and pulled the nightgown off of her.

Her eyes adjusted to the dimly lit room, the moon their only source of light. She watched him untie his drawstrings and strip off his pajama bottoms. His eyes never left her face.

From her angle his eyes were onyx, so dark yet magnetic, compelling. Her mouth suddenly went dry upon seeing his tight body silhouetted by the soft glow. He was not a bulky man, but his presence made him dangerously sexy.

His hoarse whisper broke the silence. "I have wanted to make love to you since the first time I saw you in that dingy lounge." Niko stepped closer, and quickly covered her body with his.

He looked into her eyes and she could see the spark of fire, a promise of wicked pleasures to come. He bent his head, laying a kiss on the tip of her nose, then her eyes, and, finally, he satisfyingly kissed her mouth. She kissed him back, lingering, savoring every moment.

Dove felt a lurch of excitement when he nudged her thighs apart with his hips and settled in between her legs. He deepened the kiss, taking her by surprise when the blaze of passion burned bright. With one swift motion, Niko entered her, sending rapture through her veins.

Her senses leapt to life. This was what she had been waiting for. He filled her up, and she molded to him, fitting perfectly together.

"You feel so fuckin' good." He growled against her lips.

Her heart fluttered wildly in her breast as Niko began to move, slow and sensual. She loved the sensation of his cock sliding in and out of her. Loved the feel of connecting to him so intimately.

Arching her back to take more of him, Dove reveled in the incredible sensations. She held on tightly and their bodies moved together in a harmonious rhythm. His movements increased and the faster he moved the more aroused she became.

"Harder. I need more..." she rasped.

He groaned in response to her request. "God, you're killing me. So wet, so tight." His voice was harsh, his breathing shallow.

He pounded into her and she urged him forward. Pushing into him, accepting every inch. The pressure mounted, growing until she felt a knot in her womb. Niko gripped her tighter and rotated his hips as he plunged deep inside.

The last thrust took them over the edge. Her body exploded with an intensity that left her gasping for air. A million dots of light danced in her head and when she opened her eyes to look at him, she could still see the faint sparks.

Niko collapsed on her, his body heavy yet she felt a warmth that satiated her soul. Their bodies were moist from the heated lovemaking.

This is what it's all about.

He gathered her in his arms and rolled her over until she was on top, holding her snugly against him.

"Thank you." He spoke the words with meaning.

She answered with a kiss to his neck. Dove closed her eyes, snuggling closer, enjoying the feel of his hands exploring the soft lines of her back, her waist, her hips. She squirmed and tucked her curves neatly into his own contours.

Niko let out a gentle sigh. "Have I eased your pain, siren?"

She nodded against his chest and smiled. "Completely."

"Tell me about your life Dove."

The lovemaking must have relaxed her and her normal defenses seemed to have melted away. "What would you like to know?"

"Everything." He continued caressing her back, running his fingers up and down, moving to her neck and she could not think clearly.

"I was a happy child. My parents were amazing and my sister was my best friend. We laughed a lot until one day when I had come home from school and saw my sister weeping on the floor. I knew then that the world would no longer be the same." Dove swallowed hard.

"My sister was beautiful. Graceful and kind. I loved her dearly and she promised she would never leave me." She choked on her words as the familiar emotions floated to the surface.

Niko listened silently and his hands stroking her was a peaceful calm she needed. Dove wanted to talk about Gabe. She needed to share her heartache with someone.

"I miss her. The state separated us because she was too old to be adopted. I ended up lost in the system. Pushed from one foster home to the next. You see, I wasn't of an age where couples wanted me. I was not young enough to be molded and too old to be trained."

Niko asked hesitantly, "What happened to your sister?"

"I honestly don't know. I wrote her a letter every day, then it turned to once a week, then once a year. I never received a letter back and that was the hardest thing." Dove could feel liquid slide down her cheeks and he caressed her hair to soothe the pain.

She shifted to look him in the eye. "Why? Why would she abandon me like that? Didn't she know I loved her? Needed her?"

Niko let out a heavy breath. "I'm sure she had good reasons. I don't think she wanted to hurt you. I think she would have reached out to you if she could. Sometimes obstacles are so great it's hard to break through. Maybe that's why she broke her promise."

"I want to believe that. I truly do. I would give anything in the world to see her again, have her back in my life."

Niko didn't know how to react. This would be the perfect time to tell her the truth, yet the moment was special between them and he didn't want to disrupt the bond. He hated to see what would happen if he were to tell her the truth.

His stomach churned. He didn't want to lose her, not when he had just found her. His head throbbed at the thought of Dove discovering Gabe had died a sad death. He didn't think she could have handled watching the cancer destroy such a strong and amazing woman.

Gabe had meant a lot to him, too. She was his best friend. She was the reason he was still here today and a recovered alcoholic. If Gabriella Matthews hadn't been his physical therapist after his stupid car accident he would be a lost cause. Another statistic wallowing in misery.

Niko hugged Dove closer to him.

She was the light in his dark world. A light that shined so bright and gave him hope again. He had given up after his wife and unborn child were killed in an automobile accident. He had blamed himself.

With all the money he had acquired after his father's death and his wise business investments, he had lived a charmed life. Truth be told, the first five years were the worst. He had used the modest inheritance to purchase a small computer software company. He'd worked his ass off and the end result after thousands of hours in the office garnered a huge portion of his wealth.

Niko had married his wife straight after college and those were crucial times. She had to endure the struggle to make it and along the way he had taken her for granted. Even as unintentional as it was, he had let her slip through his fingers.

"Will you help me find her?" Dove's innocent question pierced his heart.

His hand froze in mid stroke. "I'm sorry." The words came out all wrong. "I'm sorry, can you repeat that?"

"I said, will you help me find Gabe?"

He nodded, praying that the Gods would spare him this one time.

Dove leaned in and kissed him hard. "Thank you. Thank you for everything you're doing for me. For giving me a new life."

The sincerity in her voice left an ache within him.

A sudden need to claim her again seized him. Niko rolled her back around, his arousal growing inside of her. She squealed when he fondled one small globe, it's brown nipple marble hard. His mouth replaced his fingers and he cupped her breast, squeezing as he sucked.

She moaned her approval and he ran his tongue around the areola, flicking across the tip of her nipple before taking in a mouthful of flesh to worship. He gripped the firm mounds in his hands and he could feel her growing wetter.

Niko moved in and out of her while he continued laving her breasts, sucking and fondling as her pants and moans escalated. He released her breasts and entwined his fingers in hers, the other hand cupping the back of her head. He captured her lips, kissing her with a fierce hunger.

Dove responded with the same zest and he loved that about her. Their lovemaking became frenzied. His thrusts growing harder and he longed to get closer than the meeting of their bodies. He wanted to possess all of her, wanted to fill her every essence until they became one person.

He could feel his cock deep in her, and yet he wanted to bury himself deeper. This overwhelming emotion became too much to bear. This was the woman he had always meant to be with. Dove was an angel sent from above and he would stop at nothing to have her in his life forever.

The revelation left him craving more than the physical, the corporeal. He wanted her to want him in the same manner. Could she ever grow to love him? This man who had known as much loss as she had in her lifetime.

The real question was, could Dove ever forgive him for what he had done?

He couldn't hold out any longer as the energy surged through him. Niko needed to fill her with his seed again. The emotions flowed through him like warm honey and when he slid out of her then plunged back in, their bodies merged in exquisite sync with one another.

His mind screamed out 'I love you, Dove', but his voice would not allow it. Not yet.

Niko collapse on her, his body trembling and spent. He didn't know how long they stayed in this position before he started to drift, soon succumbing to the numbed sleep of a satisfied lover.

Chapter Seven

Dove stared into the crowd, her eyes locked on only one man. She sang that swan song the night Niko helped her rise from the ashes. She was a different person now. It had been ten months from the day she had left Los Angeles and her beloved home in Toluca Lake.

Her hair was longer, the thick curls now straightened by the wonders of a good flat iron. Her skin glowed from the happiness she felt in Niko's company. He had become her world, her everything.

Each passing day she learned something new about him. He loved tending to his garden and the lovely lotus blossoms he cultivated for her. His patience and support had helped her have the courage to sing again. She knew she could never want for anything because of his financial status, but she needed to make her own money.

It was the principle of it all. She was determined to be independent and he allowed her that opportunity without smothering her. Life was indeed different. Every day was a blessing.

She loved waking up in his arms, loved when he made love to her in the mornings, every chance they could. Dove couldn't help feeling giddy as a teenager whenever she thought of him. Most of all she loved the way he held her in his arms, laughed together, and enjoyed the time getting to know everything about one another.

Niko showed up for every performance even though he started getting back to work. He had acquired a failing company that developed specialized music editing software and wanted to enhance the performance to turn it around. The owner had been a close friend of his father's and through his efforts to help the man, it had helped him heal in the process.

Her voice soared as she sang because tonight she would finally tell him what was in her heart. Dove Matthews loved him and she wanted to let him know the truth. They had never spoken of those words and she was thankful. Thankful for everything he had done for her, including loving her so deeply.

Yes, she would tell him tonight after the show. Dove had asked Saban to work with the housekeepers to dress up the house for this special occasion. Everything had to be perfect.

This was not the time. The nausea was getting worse yet the thought of their creation would bring them closer together. She sang louder, more confident and happier than ever. They were going to be parents! Dove was going to be a mother. Her hormones were finding the worse time to hit. She wanted to weep from all the love growing within her. The love for Niko and their baby.

She had been so absorbed in her thoughts she hadn't seen it coming. Harry and his hounds of hell burst through the door and a scuffle ensued. One minute she was in high spirits and the next she screamed in horror.

Harry had attacked Niko and she watched as he pulled out a switchblade and plunged it into him. The bouncers pounced on Harry, but it was too late. Her Niko was sprawled on the floor, blood seeping from his wound.

Without thinking of herself, Dove ran for him. She had to stop the bleeding and tore a strip from her dress to stop the blood flow.

"Get a fuckin' ambulance!" she screamed. Hysterics breaking out.

Her perfect world had come crashing down. Everything she held dear was slipping from her hands. She cradled Niko's head in her lap, rocking without knowing her actions. It was as if she was numb. She prayed silently for the Gods to help rescue Niko as he had rescued her.

Dove watched Harry with hatred burning in her heart as the cops took him away. The rest was a blur as the paramedics took over. She protested but they led her out, blood staining her gown and her hands and all she could do was watch the flashes of white work on Niko.

Saban handed her a hot cup of tea and she refused the drink. "I'm not going to take no for an answer. You need to take care of that baby," he fussed.

Dove looked up at him from the seat next to Niko's hospital bed. She took the drink and the heat immediately warmed her palms.

Dressed in denims and a pale green dress shirt, Saban was his true self. She noticed the stubbles on his face and realized he looked like he hadn't slept in a while. Same as her, but she didn't want to miss anything when Niko woke.

The doctors said that he was in a mild coma induced from a blow to the temple and the knife wound added to the slow recovery. He thought Niko would come out of it soon but he wasn't sure when.

"It's been three days Dove. Why don't you go home and shower." Saban placed a hand on her shoulder and gave her a mothering look. "I'll sit here and if he wakes you'll bet you're the first phone call I make."

"But I can't. Not yet."

"Listen to me, Dove. You're no good to any of us if you don't go home and rest. You know the doctor told you about too much stress."

Dove placed her hand on her abdomen and knew his words rang true. She had to protect this baby. She had to make sure she wouldn't lose it under any circumstances.

"Alright." She got up slowly and hugged him tight. "Thank you for being here for us."

The tears fell so easily these days. There had been a time when they would not come and now she cried at a drop of a hat. Who was this person? Certainly not the Dove of a few months ago.

He kissed her forehead, patting her cheek. "Doll, I'll always be here for you. Rest a bit and come back this evening. Maybe draw a hot bath and relax a little."

Saban's heartfelt look of concern touched her. He was like a brother she never had and she had witnessed his loyalty firsthand. Now, three years later he had become family to her. Niko, Saban, and her unborn child were like patched work on a quilt that would become inseparable, yet complete.

"Okay. I will be back real soon to relieve you. Just remember to call if he stirs." She squeezed his hand before picking up her purse to leave.

When she arrived at the house, her part-time housekeeper, and now friend, had a hot meal cooking in the oven. Eva was a godsend. The woman was in her mid-thirties but lived a hard life. She was a battered wife who escaped to find a better life. Through a local abused women's shelter program, Dove had contracted her and she kept working for them a couple of days a week while she went to night school to get her culinary degree.

Eva's long, gorgeous ebony locks and dramatic eyes were something to be jealous about, but she sure had a mouth on her. A New Jersey native, the woman would tell you as it is and that's why she loved her friendship.

"Saban told me you'd be home so I thought I'd get something together for you before I went off to class." Eva gave her a loving hug. "You okay?"

Dove nodded, feeling exhausted from the trauma of the last three days. "I'll be fine. A nap and a hot bath should do wonders for me. I was thinking of coming back to the hospital later this evening, though."

Eva shooed her off, "What are you doing here then? March upstairs and soak that body in something sweet smelling. Your dinner should be ready in about thirty minutes. I'll be gone by then but expect you to eat."

She wasn't about to say no to the Brazilian with an Irish temper. Dove's stomach growled and she place a hand to the tiny bump. "I know, sweetie. Momma will make you nice and relaxed," she promised.

She rubbed her stomach in slow circular motions and felt the calming effects as she made her way upstairs. Ten minutes later she sank her naked body in a warm bath filled with lavender and mint. The combination was both relaxing and sensual. She loved the tingling sensation of the mint on her skin that invigorated her immediately. The faint floral fragrance enhanced the experience and she sighed, leaning her head back against the ceramic tub.

Dove woke up to the dim flicker of candles. She had dozed off sometime during singing to her baby and crying for Niko's recovery. The water was now icy and when she rose from the tub she shivered from the cold. She reached for a towel and padded through the bedroom to dress.

Dove decided on a snug pair of stretch jeans and a long-sleeved shirt since the hospital room's air conditioner tended to kick in high gear all day.

She thought a pair of socks would be appropriate to keep her little feet warm. Dove searched her drawers and found none.

"I need some socks. I can't believe I don't own a pair!" She blew out a frustrated breath.

Dove walked over to Niko's dresser and pulled out several drawers, rummaging through for any sign of socks. She pulled out the bottom drawer and dug around when her fingers touched something resembling a stack of papers. Her curiosity got the better of her and she reached, while yanking out the drawer further.

She shoved the color coordinated pairs of socks away and grabbed the stack of handwritten letters. She looked down and caught sight of a battered wooden music box. The object looked so familiar to her and an eeriness washed through her.

Dove looked down at the top of the stack and the tears streamed. Angry, hot tears burned as they tumbled down her face. These were letters written by Gabriella.

How could he?

She went mad with hurt, the piercing ache amplified and she let out a loud sob to alleviate some pain. Dove bent down and scooped up the music box. She opened up the lid and the familiar childhood lullaby sprang alive, the ballerina dancing graceful circles.

She clutched the box to her as she cried. Dove set the object down on the bed and with shaky hands she pulled out the top letter from the rubberband, ripping into it. This was dated a year ago and she didn't know if she could go through with reading it.

Dove sat on the edge of the bed, music filtering through the room. She started to read the perfect schoolteacher's penmanship.

Dear Dove, my dear sweet sister.

My time is near and I still haven't heard from you. I was told you had moved to so many different homes that it would be difficult to locate you. I've nowhere left to go. Since my time is nearing its end, I needed to tell you everything that I'm feeling before its too late.

I'm dying. The doctors tell me my cancer has spread quicker than they had imagined. Can you believe I will die before I will ever see you again, hug you again, take care of you like I had promised you. I'm sorry. So sorry you will find out this way.

If you're reading this letter, I'll be comforted with the thought my dear friend has found you at long last.

Dove couldn't read any further. The man she loved had lied to her! He didn't have the guts to tell her the truth and she had to learn this through a fucking letter that came a year after her death.

A searing pain in her abdomen made her wince, fear seizing her.

Her hands automatically flew to her growing belly. She rubbed gently and breathed deeply to control her fury and anguish.

"I will not lose you, too," she whispered. "Please stay with me."

Dove made up her mind that she had no choice but to leave. The doctors would take care of Niko, but she could no longer trust a man who could bare his soul, and withhold her only remaining family in the same breath. She tore into her closet and found a medium sized duffle bag. Overcome with the need to run, she pulled clothes from her closet, yanked out personals from her dresser and dumped whatever she could into the bag.

She grabbed the letters and music box and wrapped it in a cashmere sweater before stowing it with the rest of her belongings. Dove went to her closet and reached up to retrieve a cigar box. She pulled out the wads of hundreds she had stored from those days working in Harry's lounge. This was her modest nest egg that she had wanted to save for Niko's birthday present. She had commissioned an artist to paint her nude when her belly protruded a little more with their child. Now, she would use it to start a new life.

The cruel part of Dove wanted to hurt Niko as much as he had hurt her. She couldn't think about it anymore. She had to leave before she changed her mind. Could she ever forgive him for this? She loved him.

Don't go. Her inner voice cried.

Don't abandon Niko. He is the soulmate you sang about. He is your salvation.

"Stop it!" she yelled. "I can't bear it. I can't stay. I need to go."

Dove grabbed the duffle bag and ran down the stairs. She was grateful Eva had left so there would be no need for lies. She didn't know where she was going and she didn't know what she would do, she didn't care. Right now the only thing that mattered to her was to go as far away from Niko as possible. Dove needed time. Time to sort out her life.

Excitement ripped through her. Today was the first day of her CD signing. She glanced around at the small group of people lining the record store. Dove couldn't believe two years had passed and now the tiny music label she had signed with a year and a half ago had released her jazz album.

She turned her head and caught sight of the nanny holding her angel, her daughter Gabriella. The beautiful girl had a perfect head of shoulder length curls and amber skin. Her exotic beauty was evident even at this age.

She beamed proudly from the inside out. Gaby was the splitting image of her father, yet inherited high cheekbones and light brown eyes that belonged to Dove. A mother wouldn't be more proud. Niko would be proud.

Her heart lurched. She missed him. She couldn't deny the feelings she had for him would never fade. There were days when it had been unbearable, but she kept going. Dove needed to make her own life, to be independent and successful on her own.

Being a single mother had been the most difficult part of leaving and she had been fortunate to rent out a bedroom in Los Feliz from an old makeup artist friend who she worked with at Harry's lounge.

The struggles were many and the rewards few, but Dove wouldn't want it any other way. For the first time in her life she felt free. Free from any kind of hold on her whether it was selfish or love related. Everything she earned was from back breaking work and a desire to fulfill her dreams.

Yes, time did heal and now she could think of Niko without being angry. She was a coward. She wanted to go back to him so many times to show him their beautiful daughter, yet she became scared. Afraid he would reject her for hiding this secret.

In truth, she had been no better than him. These days she realized there was no going back. It was too late for her. Everything that mattered to her was with her now. She took one last look at Gaby and resumed signing the CD in front of her.

A hand touched hers and Dove looked up into the kind eyes belonging to Saban.

"Hi, love." He grinned, his eyes brimming with happiness at seeing her.

She squealed at the unexpected surprise. "Saban! I can't believe it's you."

Dove stood up and they embraced. She held onto him for a few seconds longer before releasing him.

"Let's meet up after." Saban grinned.

She cocked her head. "Hey, how did you find me?"

"I have my ways, sugga."

"How?" she asked firmly.

Saban gave her a sheepish look. "Kristen gave me a call the first month you returned to L.A."

"She did!" Her eyes widened. "Why are you coming here now?"

"So many questions little one." He shook his head. "I needed to keep an eye on you to know that you're alright. How do you think you had free rent the first five months!"

"You rascal. Thank you." She hugged him again. "Why don't you take Gaby off of my nanny's hands for an hour until I'm finished here and we'll talk."

"Gladly, sweets. She's a gem. Like mother, like daughter." Saban gave her a sassy wink and ran over to introduce himself to her precious daughter for the first time.

When the last of the customers received her autographed CD Dove stood up and stretched. The store clerks took charge of the cleanup and she ambled over to her baby and the man who had single-handedly won her over.

Dove watched Saban throw Gaby up in the air and she giggled with childish delight. Her little musical voice made everyone smile around them. Her daughter had developed an ear for music she wholeheartedly believed came from both herself and Niko.

She stretched out her arms and Gaby refused them, snuggling close to Saban.

"Traitor," she wrinkled her nose playfully. This earned a giggle from Gaby.

"Personally, I think she's got good taste in men." Saban smirked.

"That's fine. I'd rather it be with you than someone else." She smiled back at him.

The nanny stepped up and reached for Gaby. "I'll take her for a few minutes so you can talk." She smiled sweetly and Dove nodded in agreement.

Gaby and the nanny headed for the jazz aisle and she watched the older woman place the oversized headset over her child's tiny ears. Within seconds the girl looked to be in rapture, bobbing to the music.

Dove turned back to Saban, the wide smile intact.

"Let's take a walk," he said softly.

They strolled down the sidewalk and stopped in front of a cute sidewalk café. After grabbing their drinks they sat down on the comfortable French café style chairs. Saban moved the single decorative flower and vase aside.

"Wow, must be serious stuff." She joked.

"It is serious. Niko doesn't know I've come to see you."

"What do you mean?"

He pursed his lips. "He knows everything. You. Gaby."

"How? But..." she couldn't get the questions all out.

"We got a private investigator when we couldn't find you. Ironic that Niko came out of it the day you left. He wanted to get out of the hospital in a bad way to find you."

"He did?"

"Yes, he did. He wanted to explain about everything. He loves you Dove. He's not the kind of guy that will invade your space. He wanted you to find your own way because he knows you're stubborn." Saban reached for her hand and squeezed.

He let go, reaching into his slack's pocket to pull out a folded envelope. "You dropped this."

Dove took the letter. The same one that she had read and stopped reading that day. She could only nod and unfolded the envelope. She pulled out the letter and a dried lotus bud fell onto the table.

"Read it. Finish it," Saban urged. "I'm going to get a refill and will be back."

Dove was appreciative for the privacy. She picked up the bud and smelled the familiar scent. It reminded her of Niko and the pain started up again. An ache, a longing to touch him, be touched by him.

She placed the dried flower back on the table and unfolded the letter. Reading where she had left off the day she fled.

> *I'm dying. The doctors tell me my cancer has spread quicker than they had imagined. Can you believe I will die before I will ever see you again, hug you again, take care of you like I had promised you. I'm sorry. So sorry you will find out this way.*
>
> *If you're reading this letter, I'll be comforted with the thought my dear friend has found you at long last.*
>
> *I found him for you. Niko is perfect for you in every way. He is a good man. A kind man. He knows everything about you and even in my delirium he allows me the opportunity to re- tell stories of our youth. He is the one who can love you if you'll let him. Don't pass on this chance. Niko holds a part of me that you've always longed to hear. His friendship and love will help heal our wounds if you'll just let him into your heart.*
>
> *I know he is the one. Trust me, I would never steer you wrong. He is my angel and my gift to watch over you.*
>
> *Give him that chance. Just one last request so I may live my eternity in peace knowing you are taken care of.*
>
> *I will love you forever.*
> *Gabriella*

Saban handed her a stack of napkins and Dove took it gratefully. "I'm such a damned idiot." She dabbed at the tears and sniffed. "Do you think he would ever take me back?"

"Don't make me think you're plain stupid." He rolled his eyes. "He waited for you all this time, you think the man would be a fool enough not to take you back? How many times do I have to tell you? He loves you." Saban gave her a broad grin. "So what are you going to do about it? Sit here and mope? You can always go back and grovel."

"But Gaby, I can't leave her alone," she said in alarm.

He reached into his other pocket and pulled out a crinkled airplane ticket. "No worries. I'm known to be a superb babysitter. In fact, I've had to babysit that grumpy Niko for the last two years while you wanted to play grown-up." Saban let out a dramatic sigh.

Dove looked at the time. She had to be at the airport in less than an hour. She didn't stop to think, spontaneity pushed to the forefront and she jumped out of the chair.

She leaned down and kissed him profusely on the cheek. "Thank you. Thank you. Thank you. Take the nanny with you. She's paid up until five and then Gaby's all yours. Hope you're prepared for her mischief."

She grabbed the letter and dried bud, stuffing them in her purse before running as fast as she could for her car.

Niko bent down to pull the excess vines growing beneath the water along the inner edge of his beloved fountain. He stood up to drop the foliage in the waste bucket when a familiar tune played from behind him. Goose pimples spread down his spine and he whirled around, his hands dripping water.

She was a vision. A sight for sore eyes dressed in a baby doll dress with off the shoulder puffed sleeves and leather boots that made her damn fuckable!

Dove sauntered forward, her hips swaying suggestively. She had an innocent look on her face but personified a true siren, luring him to her. Her curls had grown out to the middle of her back and her skin held a shiny glow. She looked good. Better than ever and he was glad.

The two years had been excruciating without her and the knowledge that she carried his child without telling him made it difficult to swallow. Yet, he knew she needed the time alone. He had made sure the private investigator had photographs of his daughter in every stage of her life.

The nanny had been his. He had made sure he would know every move Dove made when it came to her and Gaby's safety. Niko would tell her later. For now, he needed to hold her, kiss her, make love to her.

70

Abstaining had been killing him slowly but he would wait a hundred years for Dove.

She stood facing him now and handed him the music box. He knew it was a peace offering and accepted the gift. He smiled and placed the wooden box gingerly on the ledge of the fountain. They didn't speak, yet their eyes said it all. The quiet communication stirred between them as he listened to her shallow breathing.

She was the most beautiful creature and he had been lost without her.

"I..." he began and she shushed him by placing a finger to his lips. "I love you."

Three simple words and that was all it took for him to lose his resolve.

He wiped his hands on his weathered jeans and reached for her, the fabric at her waist bunched up as he dragged her to him. His mouth claimed hers and the dam burst, his kisses were torrid and desperate. He sucked her lower lip, teasing the flesh, nipping, licking before plunging his tongue into her mouth. She clung to him. She accepted his kisses, matching them with her own need for him.

They hastily fumbled at their clothing, fabric swooshing everywhere and soon they were naked. He gasped at the sight of her. Under the moonlight in his very own Garden of Eden he made love to her with his eyes, roaming over her body greedily while he debated on what to do first.

"You're a goddess," he whispered hoarsely.

She smiled, that seductress' smile and he melted right there.

"Kiss me," Dove commanded and reached for him.

This was all the invitation he needed and he gathered her in his arms, kissing her like a man on death row. He could smell her feminine musk that indicated her need to be possessed by him. The scent drove him crazy and he cupped her buttocks, lifting her up and she wrapped her arms and legs around him. He carried her to the workstation and pushed her back against the table.

She parted her legs and he plunged into her, sliding into the warm, wet heat. Dove moaned, arching her back and he drove deeper into her. In and out with rapid succession. This lovemaking would be primal and punishing. There would be time later for him to worship her body and he knew that she thought the same thing.

Their lovemaking was as turbulent as their relationship, yet the calm after the storm was the most ethereal experience. His tension mounted with every thrust and he strained to keep control, yet it had been too long. He needed the quick release now.

Niko pulled back and knew she was ready, ripe for release as much as he was. With a final thrust they came together with a powerful force and energy. He felt their spirits rise together, floating back down on earth into a bed of...flowers?

Niko knew she smelled the fresh scent of the lotus blossoms as the music box played softly around them. They both turned their heads in the direction of the sound.

He didn't have to say a word but sensed that Dove knew what he was thinking.

"Gabe," they said in unison.

He looked down and his heart was so full it overflowed with passion and love for the woman in his arms.

"I love you, Dove and I swear I'll love you forever. For as long as you want me."

"Just shut up and kiss me," she complained.

"Whatever you wish." Niko meant it with all his heart.

The Universe had granted him everything he desired and he couldn't ask for anything more than having his future wife and child in his life.

Dedication

To Jax:

Because your cover smells so good.

Book List

What White Boyz Want
The Happy Birthday Book of Erotica
The Merry XXXmas Book of Erotica
Down and Dirty Volume II
Heatwave:Sizzling Sex Stories
Red Hot Erotica
Erotic Anthology:Bedtime Stories

Biography

Simone Harlow is former Catholic school girl who belives that you can never own too many Prada handbags, read too many romance novels, or be too naughty.

The Lotus Blossom Chronicles:

Concubine
By
Simone Harlow

Prologue

New Kenya
2185 A.D.

Pain shot through Nyssa Farris's body. The heel of the soldier's boot dug into the soft flesh of her neck. She could barely breathe, with fine dust trapped in her nose. Biting her lip, she refused to scream, even as the soldier's boot pressed into her skin.

Out of the corner of her eye, she could see Hasni, her lover, struggling to take every breath, his handsome face contorted with pain. A trickle of blood oozed out of his mouth. No great king should die with his face in dirt. Especially not by the hand of his own child. His end should have been as glorious as his life had been.

For the first time since his armies had been defeated in the Great War she noticed how really old he looked. How ironic that seconds before her death she saw him for what he was. Not the man who freed her from slavery, loved her and given her a child. But an old man who had given up his throne to live a quiet life raising his horses and his youngest child, and loving her. She should have never been a king's consort, much less given birth to an heir to the throne.

Blood and sand caked his umber colored skin. His dark eyes were nearly lifeless. He was dying from the rifle wound to his chest. A tear slipped down her cheek. The salt mingled with the blood from where one of the soldiers who had attacked them had slashed her face.

A hot wind from the savannah blew across the palace courtyard. The sweet fragrance of yolo blossom trees drifted past her. Her bottom lip trembled as she tripped into memory. They had planted the trees together last season when she'd told him she carried his child. They had been his gift to her. The sentimental gesture of a silly old man who could still bare fruit, he'd told her.

She had been touched.

A low keening cry of a baby shattered her descent into memory. Her baby. Makeda. Please Great One don't let them hurt my child. Take me. Take me.

Nyssa struggled to get up, but the soldier's boot kept her in place.

Unable to turn her head, she saw the boots of Princess Tarana stop in front of her.

"Let her up."

The boot scraped across her neck and then thudded behind her. The first thing she did was take a breath. Nyssa struggled to raise her head. Planting her cheek against the sand, she strained her muscles to lift her ravaged body to her feet. Dirt seeped into her bleeding wound. "Please let my daughter go."

Tarana, Hasni's daughter, kissed the baby's forehead, then smiled.

Nyssa had always hated the princess. Behind her perfect smile, there lived a snake, a cobra waiting in the leaves for the clandestine strike against its prey.

"Beg me for mercy." The princess smiled and nuzzled Makeda forehead.

Bile welled up in her throat, but she would say the words she had to. Makeda was her most precious thing. "She's just a baby. She can't harm you, Highness."

"Call me Your Majesty, whore," she corrected. Her dark eyes glittered with rage.

Did that mean that Zuri was dead? Had she killed her own brother to ascend the throne? How had Hasni not seen that her lust for power would lead to the murder of her own brother? "Please Your Majesty. Mercy for my baby."

"No," Hasni cried.

Stealing a sidelong glance at Hasni, she hoped he could forgive her. She wished she could comfort her lover, but she had to think of her own daughter first. She would do anything to see Makeda survive. "Anything, Your Majesty, she is innocent." She got down on her knees and bowed her head low, pride and hate forgotten. "Do not kill her."

"And she is my heir."

Nyssa raised her head. Thank you Great One. Her daughter would be safe. Relief washed over her. "Thank you, Majesty. Thank you."

"Stand up, Nyssa, no need to beg." She stepped over to her father and kicked him in the head. "See, Father, I can on occasion be merciful." She turned around to her guards. "You should be proud of me."

Hasni raised his head off the ground and spit out a bloody tooth. "I'll--"

Tarana kicked him again and laughed.

He fell to the ground, defeated.

Nyssa wanted to run to him, but didn't. She stared at him and for a moment saw a glimmer of understanding. She tried to smile, but the wound on her cheek hurt to much.

"Bring me the child's nurse."

One of Lion Palace guards dragged Jala forward. The old woman stumbled but kept moving. The soldier pushed her into Nyssa. To Jala's credit, she didn't show any fear.

Nyssa bowed her head. Jala did not deserve to die either. "Please, Majesty, give the old woman to your daughter," Nyssa choked out the last word. "She is a good nurse. A loyal slave. She will serve you well."

Tarana, tilted her head to the side, as if she were considering her answer. "Very well."

"Thank you." Nyssa closed her eyes. Jala would give her memory to her daughter. Nyssa saw thanks in Jala's eyes as she reached up and hugged her. "Keep me alive to her."

"I promise to keep both of her parents alive to my little one," Jala whispered.

Then Jala was yanked away and lead to the new queen's caravan.

Tarana held out her hand, and a soldier placed a dagger into her open palm.

Nyssa welcomed her end, she stared at the queen, refusing to bow her head as a last act of defiance in the face of certain death. Her child was safe, she could ask for no more from the Great One.

The queen stooped down over her father. "You should have chosen me, old man. I might have let you live." She plunged the dagger in his neck.

A spurt of blood arced in the air. Nyssa closed her eyes and bit her bottom lip so she would not scream. Her lover gone, her child gone. Her world had ended.

Nyssa waited for her turn to die. She stole a glance at the queen as she wiped her father's blood on her pants leg. She smiled at Nyssa and looked her straight into the eye. "You killed three of my personal guards, I am impressed."

Was Nyssa supposed to say thank you for the compliment?

"My father taught you to fight well. The talent should serve you well in the future."

Nyssa didn't know what to say. All she could do was stand there.

"Untie her, Captain. Make sure none of your men harm her. I want her to live for a very long time."

Chapter One

Linare Desert New Kenya
2191

Form the shade of her temporary shelter, Nyssa watched the lone figure stumble across the desert sands. The afternoon sun beat down on the man. She guessed by his height and mass it was a man, but she could be wrong. As an experienced bounty hunter she knew anyone trying to cross the desert at high noon was either an idiot or a fugitive.

The light colored clothing almost dispelled the thought that he was stupid so he must be running from something. She could see he had a water skin slung over his shoulder. This was getting better and better all the time. She stood to get a better look at the man. She figured by his stagger he had only a few hours left before the sun got to him. Then the buzzards would have a hot lunch. Pondering the matter, she wasn't sure if she wanted to leave her nice shady spot.

Generally idiots weren't her business, but fugitives, now there was another story. That dumb ass could be worth five thousand credits to her bank account. A smart girl didn't sneeze at an easy five grand.

"We gonna help?"

She turned to her partner Bakari as he took off his sand colored cap and wiped his forehead. Black curls sprang free nearly touching his ears. His nut brown skin was caked with dust just like hers. "What do you think?"

He shrugged his shoulders. "I'm kinda bored. Might be fun."

Nyssa figured if they helped that would delay her another day in answering the summons from the Queen. Stroking the neck of her horse, she thought for a few moments. What would it hurt? Not like she wanted to go and see the royal bitch anyway. Six years hadn't been a long enough time to forget her evil. Mounting her horse, she said. "We can go check it out."

"Ka ching." Bakari stood and mounted his horse preparing to follow her.

Reining her horse in the direction of the man, she smiled. If he was just an idiot, being a good Samaritan might find her a little favor with the Great One. Well then she have to start believing again.

As she reached the man he fell to his knees. Dismounting she grabbed her canteen and walked over to him.

He'd rolled over onto his stomach and looked as if he was trying to crawl away from her.

Now that almost hurt her feelings.

This guy must be desperate, she thought as she knelt down next to him. Nyssa placed a hand on his arm and found solid muscle. A tingle of awareness rushed through her. She didn't like it.

No way had this guy been out in the desert for more than a couple of days. Pulling him over onto his back, she saw a glint of steel as a dagger was inches away from her face. "Hold on, I'm not going to hurt you." She let go of his arm and grabbed his wrist easily twisting and taking the dagger from him. In his upturned hand she saw a tattoo of a cobra. The mark of the queen. She knew there would be a brand burned into his shoulder matching the tattoo on his hand. It was an old practice, one Hasni had stopped toward the end of his reign, but a practice Tarana had must have reinstated. Now why wasn't she surprised. Fucking bitch liked to mark her territory like a dog.

This wasn't an unlucky traveler, or a wanted criminal, or some random dumb ass out for a stroll, this man was an escaped slave. Not your run of mill working in the fields kind of slave either. This unlucky bastard was one of Queen Tarana's personal bond slaves. Poor guy. What he had to suffer. Smiling, she thought this was almost poetic.

Her decision made, she was going to help him and then send him on his way. With foolproof directions, as much water and food as he could carry. She'd even give him a gun and some rounds to go with. Every once in a while a girl had to be generous. Right? "This my friend is your lucky day."

His eyes widened with distrust.

Had to be the uniform, messed with them every time. She gave him back his dagger hilt first. "I'm here to help you." She patted his shoulder.

He dropped dagger at his side.

Nyssa smiled then pulled the cloth covering his face away.

The first thing she saw were the longest eyelashes she ever seen. The lashes were so long they touched his sunset kissed golden skin. This guy wasn't African like her and Bakari, he was a Norther. Euro maybe with some Arab mixed in, but definitely not native.

Gently she pushed back the rest of the rough cloth shielding his face. High cheekbones had been chapped by the desert sun but were no less beautiful. Her heart began race.   As she lifted his head wrap up, the material fell further down to expose the sweet curve of full lips. Very kissable lips. The word tantalizing came to mind. The kind of mouth that a woman would let do wicked things to her body. Biting her bottom lip, she forced herself not to sigh. She gulped, surprised she was having these kind of thoughts. The carnal kind. She hadn't had them in so long she'd forgotten she'd know how.

He opened his eyes. Emeralds.

Whoa there girl.

Staring into his pain clouded green depths, Nyssa felt her stomach clinch. Swallowing the lump in her throat, she should feel ashamed for admiring the helpless man's handsomeness, but she didn't. Not even a little. It had been a long time since she'd looked at a man with desire.

"Thank you," the raspy voice spoke.

She laughed stroking his cheek.   The rough stubble of the beginnings of a black beard scraped her palm. The heat of his skin almost burnt her hand. Was it the desert heat or was it the man, she wondered. "Don't thank me, I haven't saved you yet." Slowly she dribbled water on his mouth. Carefully, so that he wouldn't get enough to cause him pain.

His mouth opened and the water eased past his dry lips. He grabbed her wrist and tried to force her to pour more water in his mouth, but he wasn't strong enough to make her. His fingers branded into her skin possessing her. She wished she was groomed and ready for him like a real woman. Not sweaty, dirty, and tired and in the bounty hunter's uniform that was designed to hide her gender. Her body should be perfumed and softened by the finest oils. She wanted the softest silks next to her skin so it would pick up the seductive heat of her body when he touched her.

Oh this man made her want. Want things she had long pushed

aside for her solitary life. Desire things she knew were no longer hers for the asking. Funny she hadn't missed those things in a long time.

Cradling him close, she wanted to soothe him. And take away all of his pain. Like a mother would comfort a sick child. Nyssa liked the way his body felt next to hers. Maybe because she had denied herself the comfort of a man, she had no idea, but this felt so right. There was subtle heat swirling inside her that had nothing to do with the afternoon sun. It was all because of the man.

A shadow moved her and the man. "Are you going to hug him or help him?"

Bakari's voice startled her. She'd forgotten she wasn't alone. If only she had a choice. Embarrassed by her momentary weakness, she snatched her hand from the man's face. "How far to the abandoned fort from here?"

"About a twenty minute ride." Bakari squatted down next her and the man. "This guy don't look like he going to make another two seconds."

Nyssa wasn't going to let this guy die, just to spite Tarana. "He'll make it." She did feel a core of strength in him.

She poured more water on his lips. "Help me get him up and you ride there with him until it's cooler. Give him food, water and directions. And some cash."

"I don't have--"

"Pocket in your left boot." Silly boy, as if he could get one by her. "I taught you that trick." Bakari always carried cash like the rest of world wore underwear. Hell he probably took it in the shower with him.

"I'm not giving him my money."

Nyssa took a deep breath. "I'll pay you back, with interest." Tight with a credit herself, she understood his need to always have cash. "Dumb ass is going to need all the help we can spare."

Bakari sneered. "Don't we have a date to keep?"

She looked down at the man and he had passed out again, she fought the urge to stroke his face again. If Bakari weren't with her she could spend all the time she wanted with him. Damn kid. "I'll ride ahead and wait for you."

"Is he on the run?"

"Not from the law, but from her royal hiney."

"Sweet." Bakari smiled. "Why didn't you say so in the first place." He dug into his boot and pulled out a wad of bills. "You don't have to give me interest." He stuffed them in the man's hand. "Go in peace, my brother."

Nyssa couldn't help but laugh at his blatant generosity. The queen was indirectly responsible for the death of his parents. Not that Nyssa ever got the full story, but Bakari hated the bitch as much as she did. He was always willing to throw a kink into the queen's life, any way he could.

They both knew it was seriously petty, but that's all they had.

Bakari moved off to ready the horses.

Taking another look at the stranger's face, she bent over and pressed her lips to his. She just wanted one taste of him. Just a small little sample before she sent him on his way. Dry and cracked, his mouth still promised untold delights. He stirred in her arms and she pulled back almost ashamed of herself for taking advantage of him. But the taste of him had been worth the risk.

Turning her head once more, she made sure Bakari hadn't seen her kiss the escaped slave. Even though Bakari was her best friend, he would never understand. She couldn't afford to be soft. There was no place in her life for that kind of comfort. At one time yes, she let herself believe life could be sweet but not anymore.

Nyssa handed the Lion Guard her semi automatic pistols, then her cane batons. She slid the daggers out of her boots. Her machete came next and then her brass knuckles. At this rate, she would be damn near naked before she got in the throne room. Of course she couldn't go in to see the Queen armed. The temptation to kill the bitch might overwhelmed her, and her hand might slip or something.

The guard reached for Bakari's pistol, and the boy pulled back. Sixteen and he still lived in fear of being unarmed. Nyssa spent enough time on the streets of the capitol to know you didn't stay alive unless you were armed and willing to do whatever was needed to survive.

"Give it up, boy."

Bakari clutched the butt of the gun a scowl on his face. "I'll wait out here."

"No." In her heart, she knew if his life was in jeopardy she wouldn't do anything stupid. "I need you in there with me. Please."

"Fuck the Queen!"

The guard reached out to slap him.

Nyssa grabbed the guards wrist and twisted. "He's young. Cut him a break, Captain." She squeezed the pressure point on the man's wrist. Staring at him, his face remained blank. She knew he was hurting, but to the guards credit, he didn't let it show. The Bitch Queen trained her men well.

The Captain inclined his head, respect for her showing in his eyes.

She let go of the man's wrist. The last thing she wanted was the entire unit of palace guards coming down on their butts. That would just make her day. "Thanks."

Nyssa had only come for one reason. Maybe she'd catch a glimpse of her daughter. Not that she knew what her child look liked. She hoped she looked like her father. Hasni had been beautiful. Like all the royal line. "Give up the weapon. The faster we get in there and do our business, the faster we get can out."

She watched Bakari hand over his pistol. Then his dagger, his batons, and last but not least the antique semi-auto gun he had won in a poker game. "Happy?"

Nyssa took a long breath. Great One help me here. "Beyond all reason."

"You may enter." The guard opened to door.

Nyssa walked into the long room. Protocol demanded she keep her eyes on the ground, which she did. No need to antagonize the demon bitch.

"Bow your head, boy." The guard slapped the back of his head.

Bakari is going kill this guy before we even get out of here, she thought. She didn't look back, but she did hear Bakari rip off a stream of swear words that would have done their bounty hunter brethren proud.

A child's laughter echoed through the throne room, and Nyssa stopped. Dare she hope it was Makeda?

"I found you!" the child yelled.

"Of course you did, my pet. You are the smartest one in my kingdom."

Nyssa stopped. She recognized the queen's voice. Squeezing her eyes shut, she couldn't lift her head up.

"Makeda darling, come and meet a special friend of your mother's."

Her child was alive. She wanted to thank the Great One, but she had given up her faith at the same time her hope had died. She had to remain steady, the queen had probably contacted her just to taunt her with her daughter. Why had she come? Why put herself through this?

"Nyssa," Bakari hissed.

She ignored him. She could get through this. She could. She had to.

Scampering feet hurried across the tile floor. Makeda's laughter filled the room.

Nyssa wanted to look. Needed to see her baby. Her hands shook. Sweat began to form on her forehead.

"Nyssa, no need to scrape and bow for me. We are old friends."

Nyssa raised her head to see the queen settle herself on the golden throne. Tarana almost looked lost in the overpowering throne shaped like a lion's head. Her ruby colored robes only enhanced her dark cat-like beauty. Long black spiral braids surrounded her face, her smooth umber face.

Nyssa reached deep inside for calm. She had faced some of the worst criminals in her time as a licensed bounty hunter and she didn't even blink. She could do this. She trained her eyes on the queen, not looking anywhere else. "Highness, you sent for me." Oooops, that slipped.

The queen's lips thinned at the polite insult. Rage glittered in her brown eyes. "Yes, I did."

"May I ask why?

The queen held up her hands. Her long nails curved like bloodied claws. "I wanted to see you in your uniform. I'm very impressed.

You look very smart with your shiny silver badge, black tunic, and jack boots. You must have all the fugitives shaking in their shoes when they get their first peek at you. Your scar just finishes the entire outfit. I surprised you don't cover it. But I do so like it."

You should you bitch, you're responsible for it. For the first time in years, she felt self conscious about her scar. It took all her control not to reach up and try to hide it. Forcing her hands to remain at her side, Nyssa bowed her head. "Thank you."

"What the fuck?" Bakari whispered.

She looked at him out of the corner of her eye. She'd never told him about her history with the queen. As far as he was concerned, she was just a woman who felt sorry for the little slave boy and bought his freedom. She could see she would have to come clean with him as soon as they were out on here. "Just shut up," she hissed.

The queen clapped her hands together. "Makeda, come over here and say hello to Nyssa. She is one of your mother's best bounty hunters."

Makeda ran up to her, tiny black braids flying around her head. Her brown eyes widened as if in recognition. "Hello, Nyssa."

"Hello, Your Highness."

Makeda giggled, covering her mouth with her fingers. The five gold bracelets on her slender wrist jingled. "How did you know I'm the princess?"

Tears prickled in Nyssa's eyes. She blinked them away. Her daughter was so beautiful. Her sienna colored skin glowed, and she was well fed. She laughed as if she didn't have a care in the world. Good at least she was able to save her. The queen at least treated her daughter well. "I know a lot about you, princess.

Dark brown eyes widen. "Do I know you?"

"You were very young when we first met." Nyssa looked up at the smiling queen. Her hands curled into fists. "I remember you as a baby."

"Did you know my daddy?"

Nyssa tried to speak.

Makeda pouted. "He's dead."

Nyssa held her breath. The truth screamed to be told. Not knowing what to say, she remained mute. Her impulse was to grab her daughter and run, but she knew that she wouldn't make it out of the door.

The queen smiled with an expectant look on her face. "Well, Nyssa, did you know my daughter's father?"

"I knew him, Highness." I loved him. I gave him a child and in the end, I betrayed him. All that remained unsaid. It had to. Nyssa swallowed the lump in her throat and lifted her chin. "He was greatest ruler to ever live. And he was loved by his people. All of his people." Unlike the bitch who calls herself your mother.

Tarana's lips thinned to a straight line. "Yes, my little one he was much loved."

Nyssa savored her small victory.

Makeda's cupid's bow mouth turned down in a frown. "I wish I knew him."

Nyssa put her hands behind her back to stop herself from reaching out to her daughter to comfort her. Whatever was left of her soul died that moment because she couldn't alleviate her daughter's pain. "You would have loved him." As much as he loved you.

The queen stood, her rage barely concealed. "Jala," she yelled.

From a corner behind the throne, Nyssa saw her old friend hobble over. One of her arms was twisted at an odd angle, and she wore a white slaves garment. Nyssa could see burn marks on her bare legs, and she was missing several toes. She'd been tortured and maimed. What kind of life had Nyssa sentenced her old friend to? Guilt ripped her insides apart. Her knees almost buckled under her. How could she subject her friend to Tarana's brutality. Would Jala have been better off dead and not suffering under the queen's evil?

The queen sat on her throne, tapping her long nails on one of the arm rests. "Take her to the stables. It's time for her riding lesson."

Makeda squealed with delight. The joyous sound rang within Nyssa. Like her father, Makeda loved horses. For a second her heart lightened. A small part of Hasni was still alive in her. That was more than she could ask for.

Jala shuffled slowly toward her. Nyssa wanted to drop to her knees and beg her old friend's forgiveness. A tear threaten to spill over, but she fought it back. She couldn't let anyone in this room see her cry.

Although her head was angled down, Nyssa could see a smile on her face.

When Jala reached her, she lifted her head. "No tears for me, Nyssa"

Nyssa nodded her head, fighting the urge to touch her familiar face. "Thank you, old one."

Makeda took Jala's gnarled hand and pulled her toward the side entrance of the throne room. "Hurry, Jala my pony is waiting for me." Before she disappeared through the double doors, she turned and waved to Nyssa. "Bye Nyssa come see me again."

Nyssa smiled, but didn't wave back. She closed her eyes. She assigned this to her memory. When she was alone, she would savor every moment.

The pair disappeared.

The old bitterness returned and Nyssa wanted scream out her rage. So close. Tears threatened to fall again, but she bit the inside of her lip. Concentrate on the pain, she screamed at herself. Don't let this bitch break you again. The coppery taste of her blood filled her mouth. She shut her eyes as her head pounded.

"As you can see, she is very happy."

The words pierced her pain clouded brain.

"I'm a good mother to her."

Did Tarana want her to comment? Only because she doesn't know the truth. That you're a murdering, tyrannical bitch. If that bitch thought Nyssa was going to say thank you, she was wrong in every way. She was glad her daughter was unharmed. And she seemed truly happy, but how long that would last, she had no idea. Until you corrupt her and your looking at her blade at your neck. If only there was something she could do. But nothing came to mind that wouldn't risk her daughter's life. "Why am I here?"

"I have a request."

"Request my big black ass," she muttered. Nyssa couldn't believe in a palace full of guards that the bitch queen needed her for anything except a little sport. More than likely, this had to be one of her power games she liked so much. Now there was no one alive that could reign her in. "If you want me to bring back a fugitive you need to call my captain. I don't freelance."

The queen pointed to Bakari. "Can your guttersnipe be trusted?"

Nyssa looked at the teenager. Bakari rolled his eyes at her. Thankfully he kept his mouth shut. Miracles never cease. In the years since he'd been traveling with her, he'd proven himself more than once. He could keep a secret, he kept an eye on her back, and most of all he wasn't afraid to mix it up with the bad guys. Yes, she trusted him with her life. "More than most people I can name."

The queen titled her head. "I'm assuming that means you don't trust me?" Tarana gave a long dramatic sigh. "I'm your queen. I should have my subject's faith."

When had Tarana developed a sense of humor? She'd rather bed a black mamba than trust Tarana. Look how that worked out for her in past. Nyssa shrugged. "Assume as you wish, Your Highness. I have no control over that." Damn at least she sounded tough.

"Your respectful tone hides your contempt well, Nyssa." Tarana forward on her throne. "You don't have my father's protection anymore."

"And you don't disguise your threats." Cowering wouldn't get her anywhere, and she wasn't in the mood. "I'd say we're even."

"I don't have to be nice anymore. I have everything I deserve now."

Nyssa took a deep breath, remembering how close she and Bakari were to a slow painful death, if the queen wished it. "How can I serve you?"

"I want you to return what is mine."

Can I have the same deal? "I don't understand."

"My concubine has gone missing."

"So?" Bakari answered.

God she loved that kid, but that mouth was going to get him in deep shit one day.

The queen hit the arm of her throne with her open palm. "Mind your tongue, boy."

"Sorry." Bakari shrugged.

He didn't sound sorry to her, but Nyssa let it go for the moment.

"I want him back."

Okay, now she could get out of here. She wasn't picky about who she went after, but she didn't go after slaves. If they escaped their owners, she was happy to let them go, and in some cases help them along the way. She thought of the slave she run into earlier, she hoped he was nearing the border town soon and then into the Northern Empire where even the queen's hand couldn't reach him. It was one of few promises she made herself when she put on the badge, it was one of the few she'd been able to keep. "I don't hunt slaves."

The queen didn't look surprised. "So honorable. You haven't heard my terms."

"I don't need to." She turned to leave, she was heading for the first bar she found, and she wasn't leaving until she had to be carried out dead drunk. This day was too much for her to handle.

"I'll pay."

"That's nice, but I don't need your damn money." Nyssa kept walking. As she reached the door, she lifted her hand to grab the handle.

"I'll offer you a trade."

That stopped her cold. She turned around. Had she just heard what she thought she did? There was only one thing she wanted. One thing she sell herself to get back. "What are you offering?"

"Fuck no, Nyssa. You said no slaves." He put his hand on the door to stop it from closing.

"Shut up!" she hissed. If there was a hope in hell she could get Makeda back she was taking it.

He grabbed her arm, spun her around to face him and stuck a dagger in her neck. She knew he hadn't given up everything. Smiling, she was proud of him. The kid was resourceful. "I taught you everything you know, but I didn't teach you everything I know."

He narrowed his eyes.

"Look down."

By the amazed expression on his face, she knew he'd finally seen the small derringer aimed at his stomach. Not that she'd fire. Not for any reason, but he didn't need to know that at this moment.

"Now put the knife down and let me finish my business with the queen." She shoved him toward the door. "Wait outside for me."

"Kiss my ass." He said before he stomped out of the throne room.

She'd been avoiding this talk for years. Now the one person who she could count on for anything was going to see the total waste of human being she'd become. "Don't make me hunt you down, boy."

After making her way home to the old part of the city, Nyssa stared into the open courtyard of her apartment building. Her news weighed heavily on her. Wait until Bakari heard about their new assignment. What had she just gotten them into? That is, of course if he hung around to help her. She believed he would once she explained, but there was always that chance that he wouldn't. She'd deal with that when the time came.

They'd helped the queen's concubine escape. That was ironic Almost as much as it was bad. Die an unnatural, untimely slow painful dead bad. But that was the best part. Not only had she lusted after the man, helped him on his merry way, now she had to drag him back to hell. Oh there was going to be a special place in The Pits for her. There just wasn't any coming back after this one.

She touched her mouth, swearing she could still feel the caress of the man's lips. Asad's lips. That was his name. She looked up to the sky and did something she hadn't done in a long time. She talked to the Great One. "Great One how have I offended you?" Not that she expected an answer she just had to get that off her chest.

The sky was beginning to turn dark, and the stars were coming out. Bright and shiny they twinkled like gems. Staring up at the sky, she marveled at just how much of the pollution had cleared since she was child. She could actually see the stars. There was hope somewhere in the world if the sky could clear, it just wasn't aimed in her direction.

She and Bakari shared a cheap two-bedroom unit in a run down building that had survived The Great War. She sighed, wondering how many more "The Great" Wars there would be. How much more could the earth take. It's not as if the world had been rocked back into the stone ages a couple of times already.

Her landlord gave her a break on the rent because he felt safer having a couple of bounty hunters living there. She'd searched for Bakari at the bounty hunter's headquarters, but didn't find him. She figured he headed home to sulk. She prayed he hadn't left after she'd sold her soul to the devil. For six years, she didn't let herself think she'd ever have a chance to get her daughter back. And she sold her soul to get that one chance.

God, to think she'd met her next capture on the road and helped him on his way to freedom. Now she had hunt him down and bring him back to hell. Oh she wouldn't mind snaring him, but bringing him back for the queen to use as stud service was something that would damn her for all eternity. She would like to keep him for herself. This man made her remember that she was a woman. Okay, and the thought of taking from Tarana was almost too much to bear.

But at least now she had a little bit of hope. Not a shit load of trust, but she could work with that. If she were a smart girl, she'd be able to figure out how to get her daughter back, set the concubine free and screw over the queen. But one thing at a time. She thought the ability to hope for something died six years ago. Glad to know she could find something to get her through the night beside a bottle of cheap wine.

As she tethered her horse near their unit, she spotted Bakari lighting up a cigarette near a palm tree. She stomped over to him and yanked it from between his lips. "I told you to quit."

His stare contained enough venom to drop her in her tracks where she stood. "You don't have the right to tell me shit anymore."

"Get up!" She tossed the cigarette away. "We need to talk."

"You lied to me." He turned his back to her. "I'm not going with you."

She knew she'd have to explain everything to him, but right now, she was hating herself for breaking her code. "Life's a bitch ain't it."

"And so are you."

"At times." It took everything she had not to slap him across the face. She'd never hit him before; he'd already been through way too much in his young life. This was her daughter's life she was dealing with. Not some high and mighty principle that sounded good on paper. Yeah once upon a time, she thought she was Miss Morality, but that image crumbled to dust the second the right bait was hung up for her. So she was weak and had a price. She'd get over it if she got her daughter back.

He turning around and faced her. "Why are you going after a slave?" His eyes burned with anger.

"Cause the pay is right." Just tell him, her head shouted, but she still didn't want him to know she had a weakness. She was supposed to be the strong one and protect him from the big bad world.

He grunted. "That's bunch of shit. You don't give a damn about money."

The only large amount she spent in the last six years was buying him away from the bastard farmer who was working him to death. She didn't need anything money could buy. "How do you know?"

He pointed to their falling down apartment building. "You live in a damn shit hole. You put every cent you can in the bank. You are the cheapest person I know. What the hell are you saving for."

Cause one day they were gonna get the hell out of this country and that took money. Damn, she really sounded pathetic. She didn't have much to live for but him and her job. Now she was half in lust with a man she had to hand over to another woman and only sell her soul to do it. And she wanted her daughter back. "You make me sound crazy."

"I don't care why." He pulled out a pack of smokes. "I'm not going with you."

Like her, he covered everything up with a layer of toughness. They belonged together. "Yeah you are, or you wouldn't have waited."

"Why?"

"Why what?" Nyssa couldn't look at him. Instead, she focused on an abandoned oil rig, not far from their apartment building. It was left standing as a reminder of what Africa used to be. An oil whore for the rest of the world after Old Arabia dried up.

"Why did you lie to me?" For a second he looked like that little boy she'd saved so many years ago. Wanting to trust her but not sure if he could. She wanted to hug him, but knew he reject her show kindness.

She didn't want him to see the shame she kept hidden. "I want back what's mine." Then she could bury her past and then leave and be done with life for good. It didn't sound like much to ask for. Did it?

"What does she have that's yours?"

Her lip began to quiver, knowing she was about five seconds from blubbering. She fisted her hands until her nails dug into her flesh. "My daughter," her voice cracked as she fought back the tears. Damn she hadn't been this weepy since she lost Makeda. It made it her feel weak and out of control.

He sneered. "You don't have a kid."

Sucking her bottom lip in, she stared at the old oil rig, hoping for some, she didn't know, enlightenment. She forced her eyes to meet his. "You know once upon a time I had a life before you."

"Okay, where is this kid?"

"You saw her today," her voice was barely a whisper.

"No way." His eyes widened in disbelief. "You are shitting me, right?"

"No. She killed Makeda's father, took my baby and left me to live in hell." She was somewhat surprised at how few words it took to explain the situation. One would think the worst thing that had ever happened to her would take more than a few sentences. Life was strange.

Bakari leaned his head back on the tree. "Why didn't you tell me?"

"I don't like to relive the past." Mostly because she couldn't change it and it was painful.

"That still don't make it right. You and me going after a slave."

Damn couldn't he just cut her break?

His face was stone. "It don't."

Trust him to see things that clearly. What was that old saying: Two wrongs don't make a right. She knew all that, but this was her daughter. She was the one thing Nyssa could never walk away from. Did matter how she felt about what she had to do. Or that she would rather fuck the guy than bring him back to the queen in chains.

This was like getting a second chance. She would work out the details later. That had to be different than doing it for the money. She could live with the guilt if it got her daughter back. "I don't care if it's right. I don't care if I'm breaking a promise I made to you. I'm going after this slave. I going to find him, and I'm going to bring him back here. Then I'm going to take my daughter, and I'm getting out of here and out of the life."

"What about me?"

He had to ask? That hurt. She would never abandon him. Never. She loved him like he was her flesh and blood. "You always have a place with me."

"Did you replace her with me?"

She never asked herself that question. She didn't have to. She saved him, because she had to. "Never."

"Just checking." The tinge of panic cleared from his face.

She smiled, that little boy she saved was still alive and well inside. He just hid it well. "So you going with me or not?"

"Where are you going?"

"Heading toward the Northern Empire. Our boy is going home."

"So he is a Norther?

One that could get them killed if anyone knew who he really was. This was in direct violation of the Sudan Treaty. As part of the treaty, all the slaves taken from the Northern Empire were supposed to be returned years ago after the war ended. And no new slaves were to be taken. Now she didn't have to explain why she had been called. Not just anyone could be trusted to keep their mouth shut and do the job. After she found out who the man, Nyssa nearly fell over. The beautiful man that had captured her fancy was Prince Asad Kuba. Five seconds in the man's company and she would have broken laws to have him too. Funny this was the first thing she could agree with the queen on. Given a chance she would have spent a year's wages to buy him from the slave traders. "A very important one."

"Who?"

Before she answered, she made sure no one was in hearing distance. Most people were to afraid to be out after dark. Even though the city had been relatively peaceful for the last few years, old habits die hard. "Actually he's one of our new friends."

Bakari raised his eyebrows. "I'm really not understanding you."

Nyssa laughed. "So you remember that guy we helped in the

desert?"

He nodded and expression of disgust on his face. "The one you got moon-eyed over?"

"That's the one." She smiled tightly. "He's the queen's main play toy."

Bakari's mouth fell open and a shudder moved over him. "That's just wrong."

Nyssa scrubbed her face with her hands. Now for the big surprise. "Tell me about it. But that ain't all." She dropped her hands on her knees. "He not just some no name nobody, he's special."

"Who?"

"Prince Asad."

Bakari's eyes widened. "Isn't he dead?"

The Northern Empire had gone into mourning with the presumed death of the Prince. Hell from what she heard, the king of the N.E. hadn't been right since his son had been gone. "Apparently not, if he's on the run."

"Fuck me all the way to Zululand." Bakari sighed and stood up. "We're gonna die aren't we?"

All this drama over a runaway stud. "That my friend is a distinct possibility."

Chapter Two

Asad Kuba, prince of all the Northern Empires, drank in a tavern with commoners for the first time in his life. One day you go off to hunt gazelle, the next thing you know, you end up in the harem of your people's swore enemy force to copulate or die.

How the mighty had fallen.

And fallen far.

He took another sip of what these people considered a decent drink. He preferred vodka. But the Kenyans didn't have trade agreements with the Euros. Not like his father's people did. God, who the hell was he now?

His family had to think him dead, or they would have sent an army to the capital to bring him back. The bitch queen kept him hidden, the only people he was allowed to see were the slaves who attended to his grooming and the one who brought his meals. Somehow, that one slave had the cunning to have laced his meals with contraceptives. So that no matter how many times he fucked that bitch he never got her pregnant.

Allah be praised. To be connected to the hell bitch for the rest of his life would be a fate worse than death. And he would have never been able to escape without his child. For a man who grew up knowing his one duty besides ruling his nation was to produce an heir, this was the true meaning of irony. He hated irony.

He didn't even know the slave's name, and yet this man gave his life to help him escape when his plan to keep the queen childless had been found out. All he knew about the slave was that the man still bore the old king's mark, a lion's paw, tattooed on his palm; unlike the other slaves who had the queen's mark, a cobra, branded into their shoulder and tattooed on their palms.

Asad knew what was at stake. Give the queen a child, and she would hold the key to eventually ruling all of Africa and Arabia. After his father did every test to prove the baby was an heir, she would be in. Welcomed with open arms and promises. How she'd explain how she got a baby after he was supposed to dead was beyond him. The baby would eventually end up as a peace offering and herald the end of the three centuries long Kuba dynasty.

She was ambitious, evil and smart—the kind of woman a man in his position never wanted to have anywhere near him. At least he didn't have to marry her. She'd tried to put that in the Sudan Treaty, but his father never liked her or maybe he liked his son better.

He respected her father, King Hasni, and Prince Zuri, but the daughter could make any man break out in a cold sweat and run away screaming in fear.

Asad remembered the peace negotiations, when he'd first seen her at his father's court. She was flawless, dressed in the finest silks. Had she wanted an affair he might have indulged her. She flirted with him as if their marriage was assured. Instead, his father had declined the offer but gave up the Sorian Desert lands. Allah, if he'd only known what the future held in store for him. He never knew he could be used like a whore. A shiver ran through him. Only a mile and a half separated him from Arabian soil. And a trek through another desert. Three more days and he'd be home. Home with his family. Home to forget the last year of bondage.

The hairs on the back of Asad's neck rose. He turned his head slowly to scanned the crowded bar. He didn't notice anyone studying him, but he couldn't stop the sensation that he had just become someone's prey. Looking through the dirty window, he noticed the darkening sky. Thirty minutes after the sun went down, he would meet his contact who would smuggle him across the border and into his homeland. There he would be safe. And he would gather the largest army he could muster and lead them back to New Keyna and would level the city until nothing stood. He'd kill the bitch slowly enjoying every moment of her agony. And then maybe he would find his manhood again.

This tavern was a place the dregs of Africa congregated. Everyone here was hunting something. He hoped he blended in. Maybe he was just being paranoid. Escaping slavery could do that to a man. A lock of his hair fell forward as he took another drink. He pushed it back resisting the urge to take his dagger and cut it off right there. But that would draw too much attention to himself.

When he returned home, the first thing he would do was cut his hair so that he no longer had to look like a woman. Kenyans considered long hair a mark of desire. One had to have permission to grow it. Of course as official stud to the queen she insisted on his hair long. Evil bitch.

A hint of jasmine hit his nose above the stench of the tavern. Sweet and seductive, it smelled like a night in the desert palace in his homeland. The kind of night he'd almost forgotten existed. Under the notes of jasmine, he could smell a woman—an enticing, captivating, alluring woman. There was something familiar about the scent.

The tantalizing scent lingered with him since the day he was rescued by some travelers in the desert on his escape here. He couldn't remember what they looked like, he just remembered the smell. And a sultry woman's voice. That voice forced him to not give up. Maybe it was his heat addled brain, but he truly believed that voice saved his life. His senses hadn't been stirred this way in a long time. He hadn't gotten an erection without the aid of some drug since before he came to New Kenya. God, it felt good to be a real man again. Had he only had the time to indulge in her sweetness.

"You don't belong here," the soft voice whispered in his ear.

A shiver went down his spine. Asad could almost hear the smile in her voice. Something about her voice drove him deeper into memory. Something sensual and forbidden. He turned his head and stared into the most intriguing amber eyes. He couldn't see the rest of her face, but with eyes like gold and a voice like silk, she couldn't be anything but beautiful. Her scent could only be heaven sent. He smiled. "And neither do you, my lady."

"Then we should leave." She ran her hand slowly down his arm.

"You are too much of a temptation. I'm humbled before you."

Heat danced under her hand where she touched him. He wished she were nude so he could feel her skin on his. Her hands would be soft, he just knew.

"Come with me. I promise you paradise."

Could she be his contact? This woman of mystery? He hoped so. "My lady, I will regret it for the rest of my life, but I don't have the time nor do I have the funds to share your company."

She slid her hand over his forearm. "What woman would charge you for the pleasure of your company? That woman would be a fool indeed."

Her fingers were long and delicate. Her nails were painted blue, a mark of a concubine. She was a street whore, but not the coarse type that plied their trade in border towns. She was refined and obviously trained in the arts of pleasure. "You tempt me."

Her amber eyes shined with promise and her soft laughter echoed in his ears. "I hope to ensnare you. Please do not disappoint me."

She was flirting. He liked that. He wished he could figure out why she seemed known to him. How long had it been since a woman tried to attract him. He could tell she was willing to play at seduction to make the game sweeter. How she ended up on the streets and not in a Concubine House was a mystery. He wished he had the time to explore, but he needed to go home more than he needed a few hours in the arms of this seductive woman. "My lady, if I had only the time to luxuriate in your sweet charms."

"Trust me, you have the time."

Some hard and pointy object jabbed him in the back. He reached into the slit in his jacket and felt for the hilt of his dagger.

"Don't even try. Dead or alive I get paid."

She was the woman who helped him in the desert. "I know you."

"Ain't it a bitch when your past leaps up to bite you in the ass." She reached into his jacket and grasped his tightly clenched fist. "Give it up, your highness, I've seen your toy before. Don't play unless you're willing to take the game to the end."

He refused to let go of the dagger. He wasn't going back without a fight. "You helped me before?"

"I did."

His heart raced. "Do you know you're breaking the Sudan Treaty?"

"Don't care." She dug her knife a bit deeper in his skin. "Don't make me drag your royal ass out of here. Or better yet, force me to tell all these nice people who you really are. You know how your big bad daddy put a major crimp in their livelihood. I think they would carve up your carcass and ship you home piece by piece."

Asad looked around. He'd find no aid here. He just hated to let her know she had beaten him easily. "Money knows no allegiance."

She laughed and inclined her head toward the crowd. "If you had enough money, you would be in your bed by now. Trust me, none of these guys are the pay-me-after-you-deliver–the-goods type."

He gripped the bar, he wasn't going without a fight. Not back to that hell hole. "You've already collected your bounty from the Queen?"

She slipped a hand under his elbow and jerked him hard. "Maybe I got a down payment on you. Maybe I'm bringing you in because I feel like it." She yanked on him one more time, but he didn't budge. "You need to stop asking questions. Now get your pretty ass up and out of this place before I have to defend your virtue."

Asad braced his hand against the bar. She was strong as any man and nearly as tall as he was. He'd wager she was as ugly as a wildebeest once the veil and robes came off. Sweet voice and tempting smell be damned, this woman was as much of a beast as the bitch he'd escaped from. "That's not motivating me to move, bounty hunter."

She rolled her eyes and huffed. She took a step closer to him, their chests nearly touching. "These people don't give a damn about your motivations. They will slice you up first and ask questions later. And then you'd be of no interest to anyone."

He could feel the anger rolling off her. Asad knew she had won the battle of words, but they were long away from finishing the war. He hadn't even begun to fight her yet. Go now and fight later. "As you wish, my lady." With his only weapon in her hands, he would go with her for now. He would need time to form another plan. He'd escaped the palace, he could escape a low paid civil servant. He would be free again. Or he would be dead.

"Aren't you sweet?" She purred, then loosened her grip on his arm.

Blood flowed back to his hand as he took a step away from the bar, still wondering if flight was the right answer. He studied the dozen or so bodies standing between him and the bar. He'd be lucky to make it three feet. Defeated, he tried to maintain his pride.

She looped her arm through his. "Your Highness, at least look like your going to have the time of your life with me, otherwise you might hurt my feelings"

He cooled his rage. There would be time to pay her back. "I'm not that good of an actor."

She laughed again.

Considering that he wanted to kill her, he liked the sound of her laughter. Low and sultry, it almost made it seem like she was going to have a good time with him

Asad chided himself, he had followed her partner's advice to the letter, no wonder she caught up to him so easy. Part of him couldn't believe he'd been gone for less than four days, and he was tasting his freedom. Why did he think he'd covered his tracks well? "I am impressed. How did you find me in this tarvern?"

"I have friends in low places." She led him out of the tavern into the teeming streets. "I should have told you to go through the Canto Lands."

"They don't like non-believers desecrating their tribal homelands."

"How respectful of you." She scanned the streets as the vendors pulled their donkey drawn carts out of the market square. Night in the border towns was even deadlier than in the capitol. Unless you could afford pay the local law to protect you, you were shit out of luck. The people in the stone buildings began to pull down their shutters.

"Not respectful. Careful as I believe you had advised me to be."

"Don't you know this is the high holy month? They go to the jungle until the end of fasting time. I would have had a harder time tracking you through the jungle. It would have only taken you an extra week or so."

Since most of the wild life had been hunted to extinction, the Canto's resorted to cannibalism to eat. And they were exceptional hunters. He wasn't going to spend his last few moments of freedom as someone's meal no matter how much time it would have saved him.

"Thank you for catching me and making me feel like an idiot." Stepping into the dirt street, he nearly collided with a robe-clad woman. She pulled along a cart loaded with scrape metal.

"My pleasure."

Streams of people flowed around them.

The tall woman forced him around a corner into a darkened alley. A few yards ahead, he saw a teenaged boy leaning against a wall and smoking a cigarette.

The woman huffed. "Damn kid."

How low he had sunk. Captured by a woman and a child. And to think his people had at one time called him the warrior prince.

Nothing was worse for a warrior than peace; they tended to get soft and apparently stupid. What was next for him? Oh yes, now he remembered. Then they ended up the sex toy of an evil queen. Some day they'd tell this tale to children, and he would be a laughing stock for the rest of eternity. How had he ended up like this?

His father had thought the treaty he ironed out with the Kenyans nine years ago had been the crowning glory of his reign—even more important than ending slavery in his lands, driving out most of the smugglers and giving everyone a right to education.

"Put the damn cigarette out now, or I'll shove it up your ass."

Asad tightened up. For a woman with such a sweet voice, she had the disposition of a hyena.

The boy took one long drag, and then flicked it toward them. It narrowly missed the woman, but she didn't even flinch. She was tough. Again he was impressed. To be a slave catcher, she would have to be.

The boy pushed himself off the sandstone wall and walked over to them. "Happy now?"

"Beyond belief," she muttered. Then she spun Asad around and smacked him into a stone wall and slapped handcuffs on him. He heard the metallic sound of the cuffs closing and knew he was secured until they were taken off.

The woman kicked his legs apart with her feet. "Did you get the room?"

"Yeah, a real shit hole just like you told me. Couldn't you spring for something without rats? I'm not sleeping on the floor, Nyssa."

Nyssa. He liked her name. Searching his memory, he had heard the name before. It was Greek. Her skin was dark. Unlike him, if she had some Euro blood in her, it was many generations back.

She patted his legs and worked her way up his body, searching for more weapons. In a strange way, he found her touch arousing. He only hoped he wouldn't get an erection. That would make him the most pathetic man in Africa.

"I'm not in the mood for questions."

She knows her business well, thought Asad. "Do you think I'm going as easy as I did the last time, bounty hunter?" Since she had captured him already, it was more of a rhetorical question.

She pushed him against the wall and leaned in closer to him until her breasts touched his chest. "Do you think I care, concubine?"

Asad could still smell the jasmine surrounding her.

"We're going to die," the boy said.

"Keep it up the commentary kid, and I might kill you myself," she said.

"I'm so scared."

Asad, could tell the boy was not happy with the situation. He couldn't even meet his gaze. A plan began to form in his mind. Was this boy more ally then foe? Perhaps he could use that to his advantage.

She pushed him against the stone building again. "Don't tempt me."

The rough texture scraped his face. After so much time spent as the Queen's pampered whore, he'd forgotten how to be tough. In battle he'd been shot, stabbed, bitten, and he endured the pain as a mark of his right to lead men. His face really hurt, he hated being this soft. His body was oiled, waxed, and massaged. He had skin like a woman's. He couldn't go back to that life. Not again. He would rather die in this stinking alley face down in some pile of garbage than go back to that woman again.

Out of the corner of his eye, he saw the blue cloth flutter to the ground. He turned his head and saw the most sublime mouth. Full lush ruby lips were slightly parted. White teeth were just visible. Rich earth brown skin surrounded the perfect lips. He let his gaze wonder down a swan like neck to a pair of high firm breasts covered with a black tunic. Just over her heart, he saw her silver badge. She was a government bounty hunter. A beautiful enticing one. The voice matched the sultry looks. He would swear by her manner in the tavern she'd been a trained concubine. With exception of the scar, she was beautiful enough to be a sex slave. Only the most lovely of women were permitted to work in a concubine house. He could feel himself becoming aroused again.

And he hated himself for his weakness.

Chapter Three

The metal handcuffs bit into Asad's wrists. He squirmed on the hard mattress, trying to find a comfortable spot. The dingy hotel was miles above sleeping on the hard desert floor, but the desert floor had been his choice. He slept beside his men, because he fought along side them. His pride demanded he make the same sacrifices as them.

The hiss of the shower filled the room. Old pipes rattled, he turned his head and looked into the open door of the dimly lit bathroom. He could see the bounty hunter behind the glass door: nude, tall, lithe and supple. Her earth brown body was soft but strong. The curves were in all the right places, with high firm breasts. Her hair was cropped close to her head. Except for the scar on her face, she was perfect. A woman designed for pleasures of the flesh.

Had she been born a slave, she would have ended up in the Concubine House. Funny, when he'd first talked to her, she had the mannerisms and speech of one trained in the art of seduction. Most bounty hunter's he'd ever met were coarse and they were never enticing seductive women. Not that she didn't have moments of being crude. Between her and boy, they could swear in six different languages. The two of them were an interesting pair, if he'd ever seen one.

Through the glass he could see her run her hands over her body. Although her movements were hurried and efficient, he enjoyed the sensual display. His gut tightened. He fisted his hands, trying to stop the lust building in his body. He would love to have a moment to touch her skin. Her body would fascinate him for hours on end.

He shook his head. He couldn't be having these thoughts about a woman who would return him to slavery. Beautiful though she might be, she was his enemy. Jerking his arms, he tried to free himself again.

A few feet away from him, the bounty hunter had left her weapons. Had he been able to free himself, he could snatch them and go. Of course, he would take his revenge on the woman who captured him. That would be sweet. Part of him wanted to drag her home in chains, and...

"Do you really think I would have left them out if I thought you could get to them?"

He turned his head to see her wrapped in a white towel. "I had hoped." Water drops sped down her dark skin. He could smell a hint of jasmine in the air. The scent rambled around in his head, seducing him.

"Your Highness, haven't you figured out by now, I'm a tease." She dropped the towel at her feet. Even her smile held a promise of passionate indulgence. What a man wouldn't do to possess her.

Asad hissed in a breath. Even closer she was magnificent, even though most of her body was hidden in the muted lighting. Heat pooled in his gut. His cock jumped to attention and he was almost ashamed of his unbridled lust for this woman. "My lady, what would it take for you to fulfill my wishes? No price is to high for my freedom."

"Nothing you have." She raised an eyebrow. "I'm not for sale."

"Everyone has a price." Had he been in his homeland, he would pay any price for her favors.

She turned and stared at him. "Correction, I'm not for sale to you."

His fists clenched as he yanked one more time on the handcuffs. "What price is great enough for you to commit treason?"

"If I were a Norther, I'd be committing treason. I have my monarch's license to catch you and bring you back. So that makes everything okay in my book." She turned her back on him and rummaged through a battered duffle bag until she pulled out another clean uniform.

Faced with her sublime ass, his mouth went dry. Firmly muscled and high, all he could think about was cupping one of the supple cheeks. "I hope you can delude yourself with that lie, when your country is plunged into a war they can not win."

"I'll get over it."

"You will have only yourself to blame"

"That's not my problem." She pulled on a pair of black pants. "Besides, your family thinks you're dead. And I'm taking you back. So no one will never know the queen broke any treaties. Like I'm going to be spreading that news around at the bar."

Part of him liked that she wasn't self-conscience of her body. So few women were at ease with how they looked. "I will escape."

Shrugging into her black tunic, she said, "Good for you, your Highness." She buttoned the tunic up. "Just make sure it's after I get paid."

"Your friend said you were cheap. Money can't be all you care about."

"Who said money was going to change hands? If I cared about that, I take you to your father and collect a reward." She walked to the edge of the bed and sat. Slowly she eased one long leg into one of the high black boots. "I bet I could name my price for your safe return."

"What favor are you seeking? My father will grant it." he asked.

She sat just out of reach of his leg. Injuring her would do him no good, but it would make him feel better. More in control of the hell his life had become.

She looked over her shoulder at him. "That isn't your concern."

For a split second, he saw guilt in her eyes. A tiny seed of hope began to germinate in the back of his head. He could play on that. "My life is being ruined because of you. I think I deserve an answer."

"Right now I have the power of life or death over you. Do you know what that means?"

That she wasn't going to help him no matter what. But he couldn't resist from asking her. "I'm sure you will tell me, my lady."

She slid her long leg into the knee-high boots. "I don't have to answer your fucking questions. You get me?"

Loud and clear, he wanted to say but didn't. "I believe I do."

"Good." Nyssa stood. "Let's keep it that way."

Wisely, Asad shut up. He analyzed what that conversation revealed to him. She wasn't happy about what she was doing. His enemy had revealed a chink in her armor. Now all he had to do was find out what was not sitting right with her. For that, he would have to play nice with the boy. He could exploit the boy's reluctance over this assignment. To accomplish that goal he would have to make the boy his friend. "You're not making the boy sleep outside are you?"

Her mouth fell open for a second. "You can't really care where he sleeps?"

"He's a child."

Nyssa pulled out a dagger from an ornate gold and black leather sheath "That child has seen more field time than most bounty hunters. He could kill and not even raise his blood pressure. I don't coddle him. He doesn't need you to do it either."

A nice sized ruby winked at him from the ivory handle. He noticed she had taken off her concubine blue nail polish. "Forgive me, I was merely curious." An expensive blade for a simple bounty hunter. One that her graceful fingers handled with ease. This woman was deadly. He would have to remember not to push her too far.

She smiled. "Don't think you can turn him against me to help you. He may not like being here. But he dislikes failing even more."

"What made you so hard?"

Slowly, she ran a sharpening stone over the razor sharp blade. "Life."

The sound of metal on stone was beginning to grate on him. "I noticed you have a lion tattoo on your palm. You were once a slave to King Hasni."

"So what?"

"You were freed?"

"Slaves can't be bounty hunters, of course I was freed."

"Then why keep the tattoo?"

Her bottom lip trembled and her breasts rose as she took a deep breath, but she did not stop sharpening her blade. "Stop yapping."

The conversation was just getting interesting. Asad wondered if she would answer. "My lady, why keep a symbol of your bondage?"

Her hand faltered for a second. "I keep the mark out of respect."

"For who?" He already knew the answer, he just wanted her to say it.

"The man who freed me."

"The king?"

She exhaled a long breath. "Damn. Are you always this talkative?"

"How else am I to pass the time? The only person who talked to me in the last year was your queen." And she didn't say anything he wanted to hear.

She laughed. "Now that almost makes me feel sorry for you. Almost."

He smiled. He liked the sound of her laughter. He suspected she didn't laugh enough or had reason to. In another time and place, he would make sure she had many things to laugh about.

"Then free me." As soon as the words left his mouth, he knew they were a mistake.

All the laughter left her eyes, and she pointed the dagger at him. "That was very sly of you."

"I—"

She held up the blade. "Listen well, your Highness. I'm all out of sympathy. I'm not going to let you go. So thinking you can bond with me because I was once in your shoes won't work. I have a job to do, and I'm going to do it."

Asad didn't want to stop talking to her, it was almost as if he needed to, but he eyed her blade that did not need sharpening. She could hurt him without killing him if he pressed her to hard. "You have a certain manner about you. Sometimes your speech and actions speak of very formal training. You have been a concubine."

She lowered her head and continued to sharpen her dagger. "One of the best."

"How did you become a bounty hunter?"

Her chest rose. "They pay well, and I didn't have a lot of options."

She was avoiding answering him out right. Bounty hunters, although well paid, were not well thought of. "I didn't ask why, I asked how."

She shrugged. "That's the best your going to get from me at the moment."

"Take me home and you can name your price." He spoke the words softly, as if he were talking to a lover.

"You Northers talk about the evils of slavery." Her grip tightened around the hilt of the dagger. "And how every person has the right to self-determinations, but here you are offering to buy me. My price is high. No matter how much money you throw at me, you can never meet my price."

"Tell me what you want."

Nyssa shook her head. "If there was one thing I learned as a concubine, the more value you place on yourself, the more people are willing to pay to possess you. I was bought by a king. Loved by a king. Your highness, you and your promises don't impress me."

"I didn't mean to offend you." He wanted to shame her into letting him go, but he'd failed.

"Don't worry about me, your highness. I'm tougher than a few nasty comments." Nyssa sheathed her dagger and shoved it in her bag. She stood, stormed out of the room and slammed the door behind her.

Angry at himself for pushing her too far, he yanked on his handcuffs one more time, even though he knew it was useless. He hated that he cared about insulting her. He'd been so close to being free. There was no one here who would help him. He was going to return to that evil bitch, and there was nothing he could do about it.

For the first time since he'd been captured, he wished for death to free him.

Outside of the hotel room, Nyssa looked up at the stars. She wanted to cry. She hated herself. Not only because she was forcing that man back into a life he hated, one she had hated also, but she found him attractive. She was so close to bedding him. Oh Great One, what have I become.

She sat on a low stone wall encircling some withered tree she couldn't identify. The heat from the day had yet to cool outside. Somewhere in the distance, a dog barked. She hated coming to the border. Most of the buildings looked like they were one breeze from blowing down. This section of Tarken was clean, orderly and for the most part, didn't seem like it was part of New Africa. Wooden or stone building made up most of the place.

Deep in her heart, she knew the queen was lying to her, but this was the closest she'd ever thought she come to getting Makeda back. She had to take the chance, no matter what the cost.

Either take that man back or blow any chance of seeing her daughter again. Great One what a mess you have gotten me into. Hot tears ran down her face, scalding her cheeks. She couldn't even remember the last time she cried. Once tears were all she had left. She had hoped she'd moved on from being soft. Hope, she thought, is the most damning and fragile thing.

"Are you crying?"

At the sound of Bakari's voice, she turned. "No!" Quickly, she ran her fingers under her eyes to wipe the tears away, praying he hadn't seen her blubbering like a little girl. That's all she needed.

He grunted. "Yeah you are, but I'm going to pretend you're not."

She couldn't stop the smile on her face. His being in her life gave her a reason to get out of bed besides having a job. "Thanks."

He sat down beside her. "Tell me the truth, this is killing you, isn't it?"

When did this boy become so perceptive? "Yeah, but what am I supposed to do?"

He leaned back, reached into his pocket and took out his pack of cigarettes. "Hey not my issue."

She stopped herself from snatching them. At this moment, she was the last person in the entire country who had the right to get moral on anyone. It was not as if he were breaking a law or something. "In case you're interested, if the she-bitch were holding you, I'd do the same."

"I know."

The thing she liked best about Bakari was his ability to see through the bullshit the world tossed at him. The kid had a hard life for a long time. He didn't take anybody's crap if he didn't have to, hers included. "Then why are you giving me such a hard time."

"I'm a teenager." He shoved a cigarette in his mouth and lit it. "I'm supposed to." The words left his mouth on a trail of smoke.

Now that was funny. "You haven't been that young for a long time."

"True." He took another drag and blew out a perfect smoke ring. She watched it float into the air and dissipate. Great One, forgive me, I raised this smart ass. "What would you do, if you were me?"

He shrugged. "Figure out a way to get my kid and free the prince. And Great One willing be a fly on the wall to watch the queen have a meltdown."

Unless she could figure out a plan to make it as easy as he made it sound, they were stuck with plan A. No one deserved to go back to that woman, no matter what. "Why would you free the prince?"

Bakari shrugged. "Well, number one, it would irritate that bitch queen, and in my book that's reason enough."

"True, but it's a hell of risk."

He took another puff of his cigarette. "Call me crazy, but I think it might just be worth it."

Oh how she would love to get some small form of revenge on Tarana. That would almost be worth risking her life. Hers but never her daughter's or Bakari's. "You know he means nothing to me."

"Really?"

"Yes." She used to be a better liar.

"I've seen you stare down the baddest of bad and not even miss a breath, but you can't even look this guy straight in the eyes. Why is that?"

She didn't answer. Because that lie wasn't even going work for her.

"Could it be, you're feeling guilty?"

Scrubbing her face, she had hoped he hadn't noticed that this entire assignment was bothering her no end. "I'm a big girl, I'll deal with it."

"You feel like a criminal taking him back."

"Maybe I do, but I'm still going to do it."

He nodded his head in understanding. "And I'm going to help you."

"So what does that make us?"

"Desperate." Bakari dropped his cigarette and smashed it out with his boot heel.

The word rang in her head. She could smell the desperation on herself. "You ever regret staying with me since you were freed?" She knew he cared about her, but sometimes she just needed to reassure herself.

After he took another deep breath, he turned his eyes to the night sky. "Only when you used to make me take a bath every night when I was a kid. Farmer Asswipe didn't give a shit if I was clean or not."

"I care about a lot things." Lately more than she wanted to.

"We're going to get your daughter back, I promise" He slipped his arm around her shoulder. "Even if I have to kill that bitch myself."

She couldn't love him anymore had he shared her blood. "Thank you." She leaned her head on his shoulder. On rare moments like this, she felt like a real mother to him. And although she would never admit to it for fear of losing the moment, she liked that feeling. More than she thought she had a right to.

Chapter Four

Hot smooth skin touched her entire body. The sensation was like silk sliding across her bare skin. A strong back pressed up against her, molding into her breasts. Tingles of heat swirled between her legs. She hadn't let herself feel desire since Hasni died.

Moving her knee up, she encountered hard muscular thighs. Wiggling her knee, she forced herself between those long naked legs. She had to be dreaming. No man could feel this beautiful, this strong and be so helpless. No wonder Tarana wanted him for her own. What woman wouldn't want to possess such a perfect specimen to do her lustful bidding. Great One knows at this moment she wanted Asad all to herself.

Reaching out, she touched a lean hip. His skin felt like velvet under her hand. Inhaling, the strong seductive musk of a male body invaded her nostrils.

The smell of him was divine.

Her hand slid around the hip and down. She found a hard erect cock pulsing in her hand. Her gut clenched. She was feeling incredibly wanton. She wanted sex. She wanted that long thick cock buried inside her so deep, she wouldn't know where she began and he ended. She began stroking him and was rewarded with a deep satisfied groan. If she wasn't so badly mistaken he wanted her as much as she wanted him. The body next to her scooted back further, almost crushing her against the wall. She welcomed his power.

Sliding her knee up between the man's legs, she nudged his hard tight balls.

Nyssa buried her face in his neck and inhaled his scent. Against her cheek, she could feel the rapid flow of his blood and the pulse of his jugular. Moving her hand up his cock, she massaged the tip until she felt a drop of hot liquid. In between her legs she was growing moist, heavy, her sex demanding satisfaction. The ache was so delicious, she'd almost forgotten how wonderful desire could be.

Pressing her thighs together, she attempted to relieve some of the sweet ache. Ever so gently, she bit down on his skin. His entire body jerked. A taunt ass pushed back until it collided with her mound. He began to wriggle, and she relaxed her legs letting him rub against her hot sex. Sparks of pleasure rode through her entire body. She didn't doubt that she could come from him just doing this.

In the back of her mind, she knew it was the famtay root that made him want her. All concubines took the herb, ensuring that their responses to a customer were real, and that at least they would feel pleasure in the sex act. She hadn't taken it since Hasni purchased her, and knew it took at least several days to work out the body's system. The prince had been on the run for five days, so he could still be under the influence. She put her hand on him to prove this wasn't a dream. This was no dream, this was real and it was all for her.

She felt guilty taking advantage of him, but she just wanted some contact. She promised herself she wouldn't take it any further than this. She just wanted to be a real woman again, if just for a few minutes. No one touched her anymore or made her feel like a desirable woman.

Asad had awoken when she crawled in the bed him.

The old mattress sagged as she moved over him and settled herself next to the stone wall. He had expected her to sleep close, but not on top of him. Nor did he expect her to be naked. The handcuffs made it difficult, but he turned until his back faced her. He didn't want to touch her, or look at her. He should hate her.

He did, but he still wanted her.

Maybe he was more the whore than he thought. He closed his eyes and tried to force sleep to come. Well rested, he might be able to formulate a plan to get away from her and make it over the border. Beside him, he heard her deep even breathing. He turned his body around. He studied her shadowed face. Even the scar didn't detract from her beauty. No wonder she had been a concubine. The cat like eyes, the full lips, high cheek bones made her close to perfection wrapped in creamy smooth brown skin made her sublime. No wonder King Hasni wanted her for his own, she was perfect enough to charge a king's ransom.

Then she began touching him. She must have woken up. Just to torture him.

And worse, he began to react. Their bodies seemed to collide no matter where he moved. Her trembling hands traveled over his body with a gentle touch. Almost soothing. Her legs slid between his and her face sank into his neck. Allah bless a woman who knew all of a man's pleasure spots. He thought he'd died and went to heaven. And then her hand grasp his cock, and he almost lost his seed.

Frozen he wasn't sure what to do. Asad wanted her, but she was his enemy.

This had to be some kind of sin to some god.

Why not give into her? He shifted on the bed until he was on his back. Now he was exposed to her. And most surprisingly of all, he wanted to be. The queen knew how to arouse his body, but that was all. He suspected that Nyssa knew the art of delighting his soul. As well as pleasuring his body. At this moment he wouldn't exchange places with any man.

No wonder she was a king's bed partner.

She deserved no less.

It didn't matter that she was his captor or that she would hand deliver him back to a place worst than hell. In the back of his mind, he knew that if he didn't want her, she would respect his wishes, but he sensed her desperation. Her need. Her guilt. And even her desire for him. But more than that, he knew of her loneliness. He knew it so well because it was the same despair that ate at him.

He wanted her so very desperately. Maybe one night with her and he would be able face the rest of what life held in store with him.

She scooted down until she sat just above his throbbing penis. "Do you want this?"

He closed his eyes waiting for the sublime moment, she would take him. "My lady, I'm your prisoner."

Laughing, she push her body down, she took the head of shaft just inside of her. "You are so ready for me, your Highness," she said.

He could feel her heat and dampness. She wanted him as much as he desired her. The knowledge gave him a certain amount of comfort, although he would have preferred not to know. Asad fought the urge to thrust upward, to grind his hips into her and take his fill of her sweetness. "I'm a trained whore, I can perform for anyone."

Her hand covered his mouth. "No insults. Please let's forget everything else."

Good, he thought. This was just for them. He gritted his teeth. His entire body screamed for her. "Agreed." As she traced her hands up his chest, he tried to focus on not spilling his seed.

Nyssa slowly ran her fingertips down his chest. "Thank you."

Asad watched helplessly as her brown hands crept over his skin. He groaned when she massaged a hardened nipple. Expertly, she rolled her fingers around the small nub, and fire erupted on a straight line from his nipple to his engorged manhood. The sweetest of all tortures.

How she held her body in check was a miracle. He couldn't think of anything beyond getting deeper inside her. "Please," he begged and pulled on the handcuffs.

She just laughed as she leaned over and licked his nipple, then sat back on his stomach. "I'm glad you like what I'm doing."

A man would have to be long dead not find pleasure in her touch. He was thanking Allah he was alive.

She closed her eyes and touched her breasts, gently caressing each nipple with the tip of her slender fingers. She cupped her breasts and held them out to him. Then she ran her fingers down her stomach to where their bodies joined. He stared, mesmerized.

He had to have her; he lusted for her. The fact the she took genuine pleasure in what she did to him surprised him. Almost as much as it pleased him. What they were doing was more than sexual gratification, it was primal.

She raised herself off him and sat back on her haunches. He watched as her fingers glided down the smoothness of her stomach to disappear inside her. He tried to close his eyes, but she caressed herself with such abandon, he could see the pleasure fill her face.

He wanted her to stop. He needed her to continue. He loathed himself for his weakness.

Her fingers explored her inner core, and he couldn't look away. She licked her lips and moaned. He could see the engorged nub that was the center of her attentions.

"Do you like watching me?"

He did but he couldn't answer. Every word choked in his throat. She stopped and touched his chest, flicking his nipples and scooting back to clasp a warm hand about his throbbing cock. She bent over and kissed the hard tip, slipping the tip of her tongue into the tiny slit, sucking up his pre-cum. He almost lost control completely. He could feel the gathering of his seed deep inside him.

"You are a beautiful man." A bewitching smile spread across her lips. She moved over him again, nestling herself over his pulsing cock.

At the tip he was surrounded by her wet heat. He was so close to her and yet so far. What temptress game did she play with him? By Allah, he wanted this woman more than he had ever wanted his freedom. He strained against his bonds, trying to push into her.

Her hands caressed him. His mind was no longer in control. When the queen bedded him, he never lost his head. He just did what he had to and hoped it would end quickly, but with Nyssa he wanted to make love to her for hours. He didn't understand his desire for her. She was brash, sarcastic, and she was his captor, but none of that mattered.

If only his hands were free so he could touch her. When she leaned forward to lick his nipple again, he could control himself no longer and bucked, pushing himself inside her.

Nyssa groaned as her body arched. Her breasts bobbed as the tremors shook her body. "Yes."

He pushed up again, until he was completely buried inside her. She contracted around him immediately. His cock gloved inside her, he took a moment to catch his breath. Slowly, she started grinding her pelvis down on him. He lifted himself as much as he could and began grinding his hips against hers, meeting her movement for movement.

Nyssa bent over and slid her mouth on his. Her lips tasted of want and passion. He couldn't get enough of her. She eased herself up slowly, and then back down the full length of him until he was buried deep inside her again. She clenched around him, and Asad felt wetness and fire. A urgent moan escaped him. How could he so enjoy this? She was the enemy.

Nyssa moved her mouth along his cheek to his neck, then sank her teeth into his shoulder. His breathing labored, he tried not to come.

Asad was lost. He stabbed upward with fierce thrusts. "Damn you to hell."

Her hands and lips roamed over him. "I won't be there alone." She shifted her hips until they were fitted together tightly.

The rising tide of his need overtook all else. Together they found a primal rhythm. Sighs of delight came from her lips. He thrust, trying to get deeper inside her. Tight and wet, she spurred him on. The cuff scraped his wrist, but he barely felt the pain, he wished both his hands were free. He thought only of surrendering himself to such exquisite satisfaction.

Her fingers dug into his chest. Rampant pleasure shone in her eyes. She increased the tempo of her movements, sighing deep in her throat.

Then he felt a subtle shift. He could tell she was on the edge. Just a bit of nudging, and she would slip over. He began working his hips upward. His barrage of thrusts continued until she froze. One hard thrust, and her entire body began to shake. A primal scream ripped from her lips as she came.

He squeezed his eyes shut, wanting to hold the moment forever. But he couldn't. He roared to a climax. His cries of ecstasy mingled with hers, filling the room.

Nyssa collapsed on top of him. Her mouth crashed into his, and she devoured his lips. Her tongue thrust into his mouth, and she took him like they had been together for an eternity. Asad returned her fervor in equal measure. He'd never made love with such ferocity. He wanted to put his arms around her and pull her to him, but the bindings prevented him.

Exhausted, he lay cradled in her arms.

Nyssa ran a finger up and down the tight muscles of his stomach. "Thank you."

To stunned to speak, he lay under her, the sweat from their bodies mingling. He didn't understand exactly what had happened, but he knew that something had changed between them. He felt guilty thinking it, but he hoped in some way he could use it in his favor.

Chapter Five

The mid-morning sun was beating down on their backs as they rode. Nyssa reined her horse in the direction of Lake Darmac. They'd stop there and rest until the temperature dropped. They still had a week's ride to New Kenya's capitol. Seven more days, and she would have her daughter back, and her life could begin again.

She turned her head to look behind her. Prince Asad rode behind her, just in front of Bakari. When her eyes met the prince's, he scowled at her. It was the least she deserved. She'd taken advantage of him the night before. Guilt swirled inside her. Hell there was a healthy dose of shame to sit right next to the guilt.

The guilt was eating her up inside. Worse because she enjoyed making love to him. She wondered how he felt. Physically, she knew he enjoyed it, but did he think of her as he did the queen. Did he feel used like she used to? She would have stopped if he asked, but he didn't. Not that it made her feel any better.

Where the hell were her morals?

She'd never done anything like this since her days as a concubine. The day she joined the bounty hunters, she made herself a promise that she would do nothing less than honorable again. As a whore, she acted like one. Sex was her one and only weapon to survive, but Hasni had shown her she could be more than a prostitute. She was a person in her own right. And she failed him. Failed herself. Even failed her daughter. What kind of mother would she be if she couldn't help but take advantage of someone weaker than her? What lessons would she be able to teach her daughter? Much the same as the queen would teach Makeda. Damn.

How could she sleep with a man, and then betray him? She knew what he was going back to. Had circumstance been different, she wouldn't wish his fate on her worse enemy. What did Bakari tell her last night. A smart person would figure out how to rescue the prince and get her daughter back. She just needed the right plan.

But was she willing to take the risk and lose the only chance she had in the last six years to get her daughter back? Her daughter was the only thing that mattered, but then again how could she tell her daughter to do the right thing, when she couldn't do it herself.

She hated this kind of situation.

What would Tarana do to Asad once she returned him to her? Once when the Queen was a teenager, she'd seen someone else riding her horse. Just one of the stable hands exercising the neglected beast. In a jealous rage, Tarana had the horse and the slave tied to the same tree, and she had beaten the both of them with a whip.

She forced most of the stable slaves to watch the beating. The slave died of his wounds and the horse had to be put down. Had Hasni not been touring his lands, he would have stopped his daughter, and then beat her, but left on her own, she was cruel. Until the day she died, Nyssa would never forget the look of sheer triumph as she beat the slave and the horse. From that day on, Nyssa never let herself be alone in the same room with the princess.

And here she was sending that poor man back into the arms of that woman because she couldn't think of a better plan. He wouldn't survive the night.

Taking a deep breath, she gave up trying to figure out another solution. Carefully, she scanned the barren horizon, noting a dust cloud heading their way. She stopped her horse and reached into her saddlebag for her scope. Under her, the horse pranced nervously. The mare wasn't happy about whatever was heading their way. And since the riders weren't flying royal colors they could be anyone. And just anyone could be trouble. Nyssa put her scope back in the saddlebag and patted her horse's neck.

"What is it?" Bakari yelled.

Shifting in the saddle, she took another long look at the spiraling dust cloud. "Something I'm thinking we should probably avoid."

"Great!" He yelled back at her.

Her uniform would get her past most everything except the criminal element. Killing a bounty hunter was a major coup to the desert bandits. "Come on, let's head for the dunes. It's an easier place to hide." Or defend, but she left that part unsaid. No need to panic just yet. Reining her horse, she headed toward the dunes. Behind her, she could hear Bakari muttering to himself. He hated to abandon a fight, whether he had the advantage or not.

Asad headed his horse toward her. He pulled along side her and raised his cuffed wrists. "Untie me."

Did he really think that she was that dumb? She had secured his cuffs to his saddle and made sure that his mount carried the extra gear. She had given him an old nag that could keep up, but that was all. "No."

"I can fight if need be."

He was mad at her. The least he could do was plead, but nope, this guy was just plain pissed. She wanted to laugh. "You can also run."

She could tell he struggled to control his expression as he said, "Not on this ancient beast with the extra weight. She'd die before she made a mile."

She smiled. So he had guessed her motive. "We're not going to fight today; we're going to evade."

His dark eyebrow raised, mocking her. "I'm sure they had the same plan."

Now he was insulting her intelligence. "How do you know these are bandits?"

"You Kenyans are ambush fighters. Your country's army doesn't move during the day unless they have to, nor do they fight during the day if they can avoid it."

She knew that, but she wondered how he did. "How do you know that?"

"I engaged King Hasni's army many times during the Sudan War. I know how they fight. I've also fought smugglers. They don't care and use fear as a tactic."

She just assumed his service in his country's army was back behind the line where he would be safe. "And here I thought you were nothing more than just a pretty boy."

Drawing himself straight, his jaw clenched. "Once upon a time, I was a real man."

And the shame reared its ugly head again. He was all man with her last night. The heat racing through her body wasn't from the sun. She was remembering their night together making love. And from the dark fire blazing in his brown eyes, she could tell he was recalling in vivid detail their lovemaking, too. "I see." Lame as it was that was about the best she could come up with.

Asad tried to hold up his bound wrist. "I want to help you."

Nyssa bit the inside of her bottom lip. If the bandits didn't pass them by, she and Bakari would be seriously out gunned. If he was half as good as he sounded, she would need his help. But the second those cuffs came off, he'd say screw you bitch, and he'd run. It would be the smart thing. It's what she would have done. "Get behind the dunes, and I'll see if we need you to fight."

His full lips thinned, but he bowed his head in respect. "Of course, my lady."

The prince hadn't accepted this defeat gracefully. She wanted to smack him for forcing her to make the decision in the first place. Asad had to know he was wearing on her on her nerves. Like a constant drip on a stone. Water always won. It was its nature.

And she was sure she he was counting on that very fact.

Why he couldn't just shut up and do what he was told was beyond her. Good old Prince Asad just had to use every opportunity to make this more difficult for her. She wanted to shoot him in the knee, so he had something else to bitch at. Chanting her daughter's name in her head, she remembered why she had taken on this assignment.

They rode to the dunes and dug themselves in and waited for the worse to come.

Bakari and she made sure all the weapons were loaded and ready. The prince squatted down behind them, scowling as if his pouting would change her mind.

A half hour later, the dust cloud passed by them. She wanted to turn around and tell Asad, she told him so, but that wouldn't have been very nice.

Wisely, she kept them hidden another hour until she was sure the riding party was not turning back. Upset she'd wasted valuable minutes hiding, she pushed them hard to make up for lost time.

When the burning sun hit high above, she stopped them near an abandoned farm she knew about. The barn had only one wall standing or she would have gotten the horses inside. The small pond had almost dried completely up, but there was enough water for them and the horses to have a drink without wasting their own water.

They ate together without speaking. Conversation would have been too stilted and she didn't need Bakari hearing the play by play of happened last night. From time to time, she would catch the prince staring at her. When he wasn't checking her out, she would eye him under her lashes. Even dirt streaked and sweaty, he was a beautiful man. High razor sharp cheekbones, framed long lashed green eyes. A full mouth that was made for kissing frowned at her.

She wanted to yell at him to stop gawking at her, but then he'd know he was getting to her. Oh, hell no, she thought. I'm going to win this war.

"Enjoying the view, my lady."

"Screw you, prince."

"You already did."

That's it, she'd had enough of him. She stood and stomped over to the small pond. The water had cleared from the horses drinking. Damn she was hot. She wanted a bath so bad. The coldest one she could stand. She wanted to wash him off her. Maybe she was imagining it, but she still smelled him on her skin.

Nyssa squatted down and cupped the water, then rubbed the cool water over her face. Seven more days of this torture, and then she would be free of him. Water trickled down her skin cooling her off a bit. She took a deep breath. For five seconds, she found a little comfort from the heat. She wasn't going to make it.

Reaching down to get more water, she heard a small pop and a pulse bullet flew past her shoulder. She hit the dirt, rolled and grabbed for her gun out of her holster. She saw Bakari push the prince to the ground, and then take out his gun. Exposed in the open, she wished they were closer to the barn to take shelter.

The horses pulled against their reins, trying to escape. Her mare reared up almost knocking the other horses over in her bid to get away.

Horse hooves pounded on the ground as the bandits rode into their makeshift camp. She fired a round of shots, seeing two of the riders drop to the ground a few feet from her.

Another volley of shots flew past her, one grazing her upper arm.

Pain ripped through her, but she didn't drop her pistol. She'd gotten her share of flesh wounds in the past. It was no big deal.

She had to get to her other weapons. Quickly, she crawled to the horses and pulled herself up using the stir-up. Her arm was burning as she pulled out her rifle. "Bakari, uncuff him. Now!"

Bakari fired off a few more shots, and then unlocked the prince's cuffs.

Nyssa tossed the rifle to Asad. "Fuck it up, Your Highness, and I'll kill you myself."

He caught and checked the bullet chamber. Then he inclined his head toward her, turned and fired up three quick shots, bringing down a bandit. Asad turned to her and flashed her an I told you so grin.

Nyssa was impressed. So he was a little more than the queen's play toy. Then she grabbed her other pistol and tossed it to Bakari. He caught it and aimed and fired. She took another gun out of Bakari's saddle and checked to make sure the safety was off.

She aimed, and then fired. Another bandit fell. The bandit's horses reared and knocked her off her feet, her gun went flying out of her hand. Spotting it, she rolled to her knees and went after it. Before she reached it, one of the bandits on horseback galloped passed her, knocking her gun further away from her.

"Damn."

Something heavy landed on her back. A large hand grabbed her around the neck. She heard the sound of metal scraping against metal. Nothing sounded like a dagger leaving the sheath. She jammed her elbow back, hitting the soft flesh of a stomach. The hand let go, and she sprang to her feet. A glint caught her eye and a something hard hit her in the chin, she went down. Hitting the back of her heel on the ground, the blade in the sole of her boot sprang out. The bandit came at her and she lifted her sore leg until she felt it sink into deep into the man's flesh.

The bandit jumped on her, and she saw a dagger in his hand. He started pushing it toward her. Attempting to throw him off, she rolled to the side, but his knee hit her in her stomach and kept her in place. His wicked looking dagger inched closer to her. Adrenalin pumped through, but she couldn't get the fat bastard off her.

A large shadow loomed over her. A second later, she heard a soft groan and the snap of bone. The man on top of her dropped and fell to the side. Stealing a glance at him, she saw his neck turned in an odd angle. His lifeless eyes were open, staring at her. She let a sense of relief wash over her body. Good old Bakari. He always loved a hand to hand kill.

She looked up to see Asad standing over her. There was no more shooting. He was going to kill her.

He held out his hand.

She stared at the extended fingers. What the hell was he doing?

"Can you stand?"

Nyssa stared up at him, her breathing labored. He had killed the bandit instead of letting the bandit kill her. What a dumb ass.

Now she owed him her life.

Her entire mission had just changed.

Chapter Six

Asad stared up at the impressive facade of his father's palace. Graceful sand colored stones arched and curved forming domes. Ornately carved pillars stood aside arched doorways. Blue and green tiles decorated the windows.

Thank Allah nothing had changed. His knees shook. For over year he'd waited for this day.

Home.

Asad wanted to drop to his knees.

Turning, he stared at Nyssa and Bakari standing next to him. Both were dressed in the native robes of his people. They'd purchased the clothes from a camel herder en route to the palace. Although the Kenyans and his people were no longer at war, old memories ran deep, and he knew they would be safer if they blended in with the local populace.

He still had not understood why she freed him. Yes they'd made love, and he'd saved her life, but after she explained about her daughter, he still wasn't sure why she brought him home and why she was willing to risk her daughter's safety to do so. He wasn't going to question, he wasn't that much of an idiot.

Nyssa lowered the veil over her face. "I swear by all that is holy, if this plan of yours fails, I am going to kill you myself."

He smiled. She still did not trust him. "My father's army will ensure that your daughter is released."

Bakari stepped forward. "Yeah, 'cause you do not want to deal with me. I don't care who you are."

Asad was only too happy to take their comments at no more than face value. He would ensure his father's cooperation. He walked up to the guard and bowed. "I have greetings for His Majesty."

The two guards crossed their ceremonial spears to bar his entry. Asad reached up and lowered the cloth over his nose and mouth. He looked at the ibex insignia on the taller man's shoulder. One of his soldiers. "You served under me during the battle of Oranto."

The man's mouth dropped open for second. "But Highness, you

130

are dead."

Asad smiled and shook his head. "Sometimes I thought so myself."

"But--"

Asad raised his hand. "I heard the rumors myself."

Both guards dropped to one knee. "Allah be praised. You have returned."

"I can't return until you uncross your spears, Captain."

The guards stood, looked embarrassed then pulled their spears back, giving him entrance. He stepped into the palace gates and motioned for Nyssa and Bakari to follow him.

The guard followed, but Asad stopped him. "Thank you. I know the way."

It was mid morning, and his father was with his minister's in the garden courtyard as he had been every day for his entire reign.

As he walked through the entry hall, he discarded his robe. Servants stopped as they caught sight of his face. Then they kneeled. He heard the gasps of his subjects, even one old woman began to cry.

One servant took off running. "The prince lives. The prince lives!"

People began to flow into the hall. At the sight of him, they dropped to their knees and bowed low.

For a second he felt uncomfortable, even though this was the reaction he'd craved for so long. He almost felt as if he didn't deserve the respect of his people. Not after what he'd been forced to do.

Out of the corner of his eye, he saw an emerald blur approach him. He turned and came face to face with his beloved mother.

"My son. My son." Tears streamed down her face. He took his mother in his arms and pressed his face in her hair. She smelled of vanilla and roses. She smelled like home. It took him a second to realize just how much he'd missed this smell.

Her arms tightened around him. Over her head, he saw his father walking into the entry hall, a bevy of servant and ministers on his tail.

His father's face looked old. As he cleared the giant arch, he stopped.

Asad could see his entire body shake. One of his personal

attendants reached out and gently grabbed his father's arm. His father shook him off and walked slowly over to him. Asad smiled and held out one of his arms.

As he father moved into his embrace, he felt a sense of peace he never thought he would feel again.

His father lifted his tear stained face. "Where have you been?"

"Before I tell you, that woman and boy standing behind me are responsible for bringing me home to you."

A tear fell down his father's cheek. "However I can reward them, it will be done."

"For now just thank them."

His father left his arms and walked to Nyssa and did something Asad had never seen him do except in the family mosque. His father slowly got to his knees and bent low over Nyssa's feet and kissed her boots.

A shocked gasp went through the crowd. He stood and took Nyssa face in his hands. "No price is too great for the gift you bring to an old man."

Nyssa mouth just moved up and down, but no sound came out. She looked to him, panic written all over her face.

Asad decided he liked her silent.

Asad opened the door to the guest room his mother had assigned to Nyssa. "Are you comfortable?" He knew the question was moot, but he didn't know what else to say to her.

She sat on the windowsill, staring off into the distance. "Nice palace you got here. I can see why you wanted to come home."

He shrugged. "I've missed my favorite pillow." His old humor had returned.

Turning to face him, she rolled her eyes. "That's not what I meant."

"I know." He smiled. "You don't have much of a sense of humor."

She rotated back to looking out of the window. "I can't afford one."

"Pity. You should laugh more."

Walking into the room further, he studied her profile. The long scar nearly touched the corner of her mouth, giving her a wicked smile. Part of him wished he could fix the damage for her, but he knew she would refuse. In a strange way, she wore the scar like a badge of honor. "In a weeks time, you'll have your daughter back."

She said nothing.

Didn't she believe him? "My father's pride would prevent him from doing anything less."

Nyssa took a deep breath and closed her eyes refusing to look at him. "I'm sure your father intends to keep his end of the bargain. I just don't think Makeda is going to be so easy to take from the queen."

In his head, the deed was done. This is how he fought a battle, and this was how he would get her daughter back. All that was left was to carry out the deed. "My father leads the strongest army between our two nations. An army that is loyal to him and loyal to me. An army which is looking forward to battle again."

Nyssa leaned her head back on the window. "Tarana's army may not love her, but they do serve her."

"Why won't you look at me?"

"Because I'm ashamed." She lifted her feet up and pulled her knees to her chest.

His feet took him across the room until he was standing next to her. "You have nothing to be ashamed of." And he truly believed this. She had done what she thought she must to survive and get her daughter back. He hoped if he were faced with the same choices he would do no less.

"I broke a promise to a friend. I used you like a concubine. I committed treason, and I'm going to take my daughter away from the only home she's ever known. I have plenty to be ashamed of."

"Bakari forgave you. As for treason, you are doing what is right instead of what you were ordered to do. That takes courage."

Her lips quirked. "Two out of four. I'll sleep easy tonight."

Why didn't she believe him? He did understand. "When your daughter is old enough to understand the truth, she will forgive you. I don't have children, but I know my father would have sold his soul ensure my safe return."

"And what about you, Prince Asad." She trained her narrowed eyes on him.

His hands began to sweat. Didn't she have any idea what she did to him? Just being near her, he wanted her again. "What do you mean?"

"Do you forgive me?"

His throat was dry. He wanted to say yes, but he couldn't talk. She made him feel like a man again. She gave him back his respect when she trusted him to help her fight. And he wanted her.

"Well?"

He licked his bottom lip. It was hard to concentrate when she looked at him with all that fire burning in her eyes. "There is nothing to forgive." There he'd said it, and he really did believe it.

"I know I didn't rape you, but I took advantage of the situation."

He was fighting the urge to touch her. He suspected she would rebuff the contact. "No, you didn't."

"I'm not saying you didn't have a good time. The herb guarantees that."

Asad couldn't stop the smile on his face. "I haven't been taking the herb for a while."

Mouth dropped open for a second. "What?"

"The queen's been a bit preoccupied to visit. Probably planning her take over of my homelands." He shrugged his shoulders, liking the fact that he surprised her. "My keeper stopped feeding me the herb several weeks ago."

"Someone in the palace was helping you?"

"I admire the way you are able to shift the conversation to a less emotional topic."

She blew out a long breath and turned away from him. "What do you want me say? You liked fucking me. A lot of men did. What's special about that?"

"Let me make it easier for you to understand; I wanted to fuck you," he said with a harshness he hadn't intended. The possibility that he was nothing more than a "fuck" to her angered him. The idea that he actually cared, scared him.

"I was still wrong."

"Why?"

Leaning her head back on the windowsill, she was silent for a moment. "Because I spent a lot of time having sex with men I couldn't stand. I knew what your life was like, and I still made you have sex with me. I was even going to march you back to the bitch queen and walk away."

Sitting next to her, he wanted to take her in his arms and comfort her, but he knew she'd rebuff him. "My life was never as bad as yours. I never really thought about slavery other than that my father didn't approve of it. When he became king, he ended slavery. I still spent the majority of my life having someone else get me a glass a water because they had to, not because they like me."

"Your father pays his servants. There is a big difference between being a slave and being a servant. I serve the queen, but for brief time I was her father's slave."

"And yet you still loved him?" After saying the words, he hated how jealous he felt for a dead man.

"He was good to me and my daughter."

"That's not the only reason you loved him. Or still love him."

Nyssa shook her hand in front of her face. "Don't try and get into my head. I brought you back here because you saved my ass, and I feel guilty. I figured that was the least I owed you."

"Why are you angry?"

"I'm not angry, I'm scared."

"You're safe here." He put his hand on her knee.

She pushed his hand off and scowled at him. "I'm afraid I'm not going to get my daughter back. I'm scared that if I do, she'll hate me for the rest of my life. I'm afraid if I try to get her back and fail, Tarana will take her revenge by killing her. And I'm scared because I like you more than I should. Are you happy now? Did you enjoy seeing me crack?"

Yes he did, because it made her seem more human, but he would lie to make her feel better. "No, I didn't. Why would you think I would?"

"Because I was a bitch to you."

"You were doing what you thought you had to do."

"Stop being so understanding."

He fought a smile. "Actually, I'm being honest."

"Why are you here anyway? Don't you have some princely business to take care of?"

He had a million things he could be doing, but he wanted to be with her. "You're the only business I want to take care of at the moment."

"I don't get it?"

"Yes you do."

Nyssa shrugged. "What?"

"I'm here because I want you."

Her eyes mirrored her shock. "Well I don't want you." She pointed to the door. "So go."

But behind that disbelief, he saw her desire too. That pleased him. "I think you do."

Nyssa rolled her eyes. "Maybe I do, but I'm not going to do anything about it."

He smiled and stood. "You don't have to."

"You confuse me."

Another thing that pleased him. "How so?"

She folded her arms over her chest. "I spent a lifetime reading men so I could give them what they wanted so they would go on their merry way and leave me alone. I have no idea what you want except revenge against the queen and to get in my pants."

He shrugged. For all his breeding and highborn ways, he was a simple man. She excited him. Challenged him. She talked to him like a man, not a prince of the blood. She had no idea how much he liked and respected her for that. "For the moment, all I want is to take you to bed."

She seemed skeptical. "The other night was the first time I've been with anyone since Hasni died. I thought I would feel as if I was betraying him. I didn't. Part of me thinks I'm more whore than I thought I was."

He reached out and cupped her cheek. "A concubine by no choice of your own, but never a whore."

"Stop wrapping everything up in a nice package." Nyssa tried to pull away from him. "I forgot everything I believed in for my own gain. That's a whore."

"If my child's freedom were at stake, I would betray everything."

Shaking her head, she frowned. "Not you."

He rubbed his thumb on her soft cheek, enjoying the feel of her skin. "I'm a man not a martyr."

"Why are you going to help me?"

"It's the right thing to do."

Nyssa put her hand on top of his. "You're pretty good at that."

Asad reached up and stroked her cheek. He would never get bored with the silk of her skin. "And a small part of me wants to impress you."

She laughed and looked down at his crotch. "Well not so small."

"Come to bed."

"You don't have to sleep with me because your grateful. You're father has given Bakari and me a lot of money. You're debt is paid."

Dear Allah, why did he have to want a woman who was so stubborn? Because that what made her so exciting. "After we save the girl, killed the evil queen and free your people, I intend to make you my wife."

Her mouth fell open.

Well he was just as surprised at the words that had come out of his mouth. Did he really just propose to her? "I like you quiet."

"You can't marry me." She pushed his hand off her cheek and stood. "I'm a bounty hunter. A foreigner. I was a slave. You need a nice noble woman. From a nice noble family. You've got plenty to chose from around here." Shaking her hand, she walked away from him.

The sheer unadulterated panic in her eyes rather amused him. "Nice women bore me. I want you."

"No."

He grabbed her around the waist, threw her over his shoulder and headed toward the large bed. "I'm the prince. I get what I want. Haven't you figured that out yet?"

Her back hit the mattress. "Your Highness, I'm not one of your subjects."

He got on the bed and trapped her body between his powerful

thighs. "You are on my lands in my home, I always get what I want. Those are my rules." He grabbed her wrists and held her still.

She tried to buck him off her, but he didn't even budge. "No."

He brought her wrists together and held them with one large hand. With his free hand, he untied the sash of her robe and pushed the silky fabric aside. "Woman, I'm offering you my name, and my kingdom. I will not be tossed aside."

"It's not enough."

He should have known with her it wouldn't be. "What more could you want?" Part of him was glad that it wasn't. She was right she was worth a high price. One he was more than willing to pay to keep her.

A tear slide down her cheek. "A man who will love my daughter as his own."

"I will spoil her rotten and be the perfect father." As soon as the words left his mouth he knew that he had spoken the truth.

Her eyes held his, and the look inside their depths was almost pleading. "I want your heart."

Ahh so her truth had finally been spoken. Silly woman she owned him body and soul. "You've had that for days now." He leaned over and kissed her. His lips gently parted hers, and his tongue slipped between her teeth.

She relaxed under him. His mouth caressed hers as his long hair slid across her cheek. As his mouth explored her mouth, his hand freed her of the rest of her clothing.

Her body exposed, he lifted his head and let go of her wrist. This was the first time he'd seen her nude body up close. He ran the tips of his fingers down her chest over the curve of her breast. One long fingertip grazed her hardened nipple, and she moaned. Her body arced up until her sex touched his already erect shaft.

Asad closed his eyes and savored the sensation.

Nyssa reached up, snaked her hand around his neck and brought his mouth back down to hers. She stopped just as his lips neared her. "Swear to me on your life, my daughter will be safe."

"I would die for her and for you."

"You'd better not." She yanked him down and gave him a hard kiss.

Asad took off his robe as they kissed. He lowered his body until skin touched skin. Settling on top of her, he fought off the urge to plunge deep inside her. He wanted to make love to her, not take her like an animal. She deserved his tenderness and his care.

Gliding his hand down her flat stomach, he felt her quiver under his touch. He like the sensation. Continuing lower, he slid his hand between her legs and touched her sex. She was wet and warm for him. She arched her body, and his finger slipped inside her. Almost immediately, he felt her clamp around him.

Slowly, he moved his finger inside her. Slowly he flicked her clit with his thumb. The hard bud swelled, and he heard her moan under his lips. Shifting, he moved to lay by her side without taking his finger out of her moist depths. He started shaking as he broke the kiss and lifted his head.

"Take me now."

"I want to explore you."

"Later. I have to have you inside me."

"Demanding woman."

"Damn right."

He rolled on top of her. Her long legs slid around his hips. He lifted himself up over her. His shaft was poised just over her sex. "I wanted to go slow."

"Just love me."

"Until my very last breath." He lowered himself to slide inside of her.

Her heat welcomed him. Nyssa internal muscles tightened around him, gripping him. Their bodies had truly become one in the same. Stroking in and out of her, he reveled in every shudder of her body.

Nyssa ran her hands down his chest, then his stomach until she found the spot where their bodies were joined. She touched his hardness, and a spike of pleasure ran through him. Her vaginal muscle gripped him, and she began to work them over his straining shaft. He felt as if he was going to explode inside her. He tried to pull back, but she wrapped her legs around him, pushing her heels into the small of his back.

"Let me love you," he whispered.

"No."

"Woman." His voice was tight as she milked him, and he couldn't catch his breath. She ground herself against him as she crashed over the edge. He soon followed.

Laying on top of her, he made himself a vow. He would free them forever from the queen's grip or he would die trying.

Chapter Seven

Nyssa wiped the sweat from her palms on her trousers. Asad stood next to her in the queen's throne room. He was secured in handcuffs and ad the nerve to looked calm. "Are you sure everyone is in place?" Nyssa was surprised at how many of the queen's court were ready to betray her.

The last few days, they were able to slip in several hundred of Asad's soldiers. They had even been able to get the king and his royal entourage inside the city limits to pay his ally a well-planned impromptu visit.

He signed. "Yes. The same as they were when you asked me five minutes ago."

Out of the corner of her eye, she spied Bakari cleaning his nails with the tip of small dagger. He raised his head. "I'm cool."

Why was she the only one who was nervous? "Look this has to go off—"

"My lady, I'm the one in chains. Please let me be the one to look nervous."

She took a deep breath, remembering she had delivered hundreds of prisoner to justice. This wasn't anything new fresh and exciting for her. "You're acting like your getting ready to attend a state dinner."

"We are. Tonight we eat at the queen's table." He snickered. "Without the queen."

She heard the laughter in his voice and wanted to smack him. "Will you keep it down?"

"Will you stop acting guilty?"

She scrubbed her face, afraid she might yell. "I'm way past guilty."

"You are going to give yourself a heart attack."

Before she could answer, she heard a peal of childish laughter. Her gut tightened; she wasn't prepared to risk her daughter's safety during a coup.

Nyssa took a deep breath. She had no choice. How she would explain all this to her daughter, she hadn't figured out yet, but at least she would have chance to try.

The queen walked into the throne room. Her long red robes billowed behind her. "Nyssa, I had almost given up hope of your safe return."

Nyssa bowed low. "I always keep my bargains."

"How well you serve me." Tarana walked closer to Asad. "Look, daughter, my special friend has come back to me."

"Nyssa." The girl smiled up at her.

Nyssa couldn't help herself, she reached out and palmed the girl's cheek. "Princess."

"Don't touch a royal bounty hunter."

Nyssa narrowed her eyes and withdrew her hand. It was true, the queen had no intention of keeping her end of the deal. "Many pardons, Highness."

"You are forgiven, this time." The queen reached out and caressed Asad chest. "Oh, how I have missed you in my bed, my love."

Asad turned his head away, an expression of disgust on his face.

Nyssa had to put her hands behind her back to stop herself from clawing the woman's eyes out. "I want my payment."

"No," she shook her head. "Get out before I have you arrested."

Nyssa whipped a gun out from under her tunic and held it to Asad's head. "Bitch, I want what's mine."

"Guards!"

The double doors flung open.

The Northern Empire's king walked through the doors, surround by his guards dressed in Kenyan uniforms. "My old friend, Tarana. Greetings"

The queen's face contoured with rage. "You betrayed me whore." She swung her hand out.

Nyssa grabbed her wrist. "As if you were going to hold up your end of the deal." She twisted the queen's wrist.

"Momma!" Makeda ran to the queen.

Nyssa dropped the queen's wrist and tried to catch the girl.

The queen picked up the girl and held her to her chest. "Don't worry, I'll protect us." She withdrew a dagger and held it up.

The emperor's guard rushed her.

Nyssa held up her arm. "No one touches them."

The guards stopped, looking confused.

Asad came to her side. "No one touches the queen."

"I will not surrender my throne."

Asad stepped closer to the queen. "You broke the Sudan treaty. My armies are poised to march on your city. Do you think you can risk war?"

Tarana put Makeda down, but still held her hand. "I want a trial."

"No!" the king shouted.

The queen pounded on her chest with her free hand. "It is my right."

The king took a long breath. "I'm offering you exile. If you go to trial, you will be found guilty, tortured, and then executed. Do you wish the child to see your end in such a manner? That is the only reason, I'm offering you exile."

Tarana held up her chin her eyes glittering with defiance. "My people will not stand for it."

The king laughed. "Your people helped me capture you."

"I demand trial by combat."

The king began to take off his robe, but Asad stepped forward. "I want to kill her."

The king opened his mouth.

Nyssa put her hand on the king's arm. "Sorry, boys, she's all mine."

Everyone in the room turned to face Nyssa. She swallowed the huge lump in her throat.

Asad moved in front of her. "No."

She refused to be persuaded. This was a long time coming. "No one here has had their life more fucked over by this bitch. She killed my king, she took away my child, and punished me by letting me live. I want justice."

Asad ran a finger down her cheek. "I will not risk you, my love."

She leaned into his touch. "I'm no more at risk than you are."

"I'm a trained solider."

She couldn't let the man she loved fight her battles no matter how much she wanted him to. "Who has been confined to a gilded cage for a long time. I've fought everyday with people who hate me more than she does." She smiled. "I'm going to kill her."

Asad leaned his toward hers. "Do you want your daughter to see that side of you?"

"I wasn't going to let her stay." Nyssa looked around and spotted Jala. She motioned her over. "Please take her out of here."

"No, my daughter stays."

Nyssa shook her head. "No, my daughter doesn't."

Tarena smiled. "You haven't beaten me yet whore. She's mine by law."

Nyssa knew the law. Tarana was right. Until the queen was defeated or tried, she still was the final word. "Fine, let's do this, bitch."

"No." Asad grabbed her upper arm. "No woman is fighting for me."

She wanted to laugh at his silly brand of chivalry. "No man is going to finish my battle."

"Son," the king stepped between them, "she is a Kenyan. Who better to kill a traitor?"

Asad stared at her. The love burning in his eyes. "Be quick."

Nyssa smiled. "I just have to be good." Then she snaked her arm around his neck and pulled him down for a quick kiss. His lips were firm and tasted of promise. She'd win just to kiss him again. After she let him go, she turned to the queen. "You ready?"

Sheer fury burned in Tarana's eyes. "I win and you leave my country. And I hope you are prepared for war, you old bastard." She didn't even bother to look at the king.

The king raised one of his bushy eyebrows. "Had it been you instead of your father, I wouldn't have stopped until I drove your nation into the ground."

Tarana spit at the king's feet. "Had I waged war against you old man, I'd have your empire."

Nyssa shook her head, that woman just didn't know when to quit and call it a day.

Bakari held out his blade to Nyssa. "Make the bitch shut up, or I'm gonna miss lunch."

She took it. "You have no patience."

Barkari snorted. "Not for stupid shit."

Nyssa laughed.

The crowd formed a circle around the two of them. The queen stripped down to her tunic and trousers.

Nyssa handed all of her guns to Bakari. She bent over and took off her boots.

The queen put her hands on her hips. "Are you going to kill me with your stench?"

Nyssa hit the release button on one of the heels and the curved blade slide out from the toe.

The crowd gasped.

Nyssa rotated her shoulders loosening her muscles. She turned to look at Asad. He walked up to her, took her in his arms and kissed her hard.

"Hurry."

"Nope. This is going to be a pleasure."

"As you wish."

Before Nyssa could turn around to face the queen, something hard hit her back. Nyssa flew into the crowd. Kicking back, she made contact with the queen's stomach. The woman slid back and Nyssa turned.

The queen flew at her again, and Nyssa danced out of the way.

The queen swiped her blade in front of Nyssa's face, missing her by a scant inch. Nyssa hooked her foot behind the queen's knee, tripping her.

The queen stumbled but didn't fall. She righted herself and drew herself up.

Nyssa swung her fist, connecting with Tarana's jaw. Then she threw a punch that landed in her stomach.

Tarana slashed her blade up and Nyssa grabbed her wrist and twisted the queen's wrist. The queen went to her knees and dropped the blade.

Makeda screamed, and Nyssa rotated to face her daughter. Thankfully, Jala held her in her good arm, even though the little girl was thrashing in the old woman's arms. Nyssa walked over to the dagger and kicked it away. She fisted a handful of the queen's hair and turned her face up to her. She put her dagger in the waistband of her trousers. "I'm going to give you the choice you never gave me. Pack up your crap and hit the road. All you do is leave Makeda with me."

"Never." The queen spit blood at Nyssa feet.

"Okay." Nyssa lifted the woman by her hair until she stood. Then Nyssa smacked her across the face. "That's for your father." She smacked her again. "That's for what you did to my man." She balled her fist and hit her in the jaw. "That is for taking my daughter away."

Blood gushed from the queen's mouth.

Nyssa withdrew her blade and dragged the tip down the queen's cheek. "That's for me." A trail of blood dripped down her flawless brown skin. "Now get your ass up and leave before I finish the job." She lowered her dagger, turned her back and walked away.

The crowd stared in stunned silence.

A few seconds passed. She won. Her enemy was finally defeated.

"Momma!" Makeda's tiny feet echoed over the tiles.

Nyssa turned just in time to see her daughter fly into the arms of the queen.

As the queen's arm moved up Makeda's back, Nyssa saw the glitter of steel.

"You will never have her, whore." The queen raised her dagger, Makeda screamed.

Nyssa reached for her dagger as something sailed passed her ear.

The dagger struck the queen between her eyes.

Makeda screamed again, and Nyssa raced over to catch her daughter before she fell from the dead queen's arms.

Nyssa grabbed her daughter as the queen slid to the ground. She turned to see Asad grinning. "I told you woman, she was my kill."

The queen's chief minister stepped forward and toed the queen's body. "The queen is dead." He looked a Makeda, and then went to one knee. "Long live the queen."

Nyssa watched the powerful king of the Northern Empire show her daughter the fine art of building a sand castle. In two days, they would have Makeda's coronation. How had a former concubine come to this point in her life?

"Come back to bed."

She turned and looked at Asad lying naked on crimson sheets. "I will in a minute."

"Only old men and little girls have to be up this early in morning."

"I just like watching Makeda with your father. They have the most intense conversations. What could they be talking about?"

She heard him sigh and the bed covers rustle as he got up. A few seconds later, he was at her side. "He's teaching her how to be queen. He did the same with me."

"Did you learn your lessons well?"

"We shall see."

She leaned her head on his broad chest, still not believing that Asad's father was stepping aside to let his son rule. It had taken Makeda awhile to accept as her mother, but once Jala told her the truth, Makeda let herself believe. There was still a bit shyness, but Nyssa hoped that would melt away as soon as mother and daughter got to each other better. Who the little princess really adored was Asad's father. The old king had been very good about bridging the gap between them. For that she would be eternally grateful.

"I'm not ready to be the mother of queen, much less a queen myself."

Asad slipped an arm around her waist. "You'll do fine."

Nyssa gripped his hand marveling at the strength she felt in him. "Because I have you."

"You have lived the life of most of your subjects. I've always had privilege."

A slave, a bounty hunter and now nobility. How she got here she'd never know. "What if, I—"

"I love you. The people love you. And Makeda is growing to love you. What more do you need?"

She turned and looked at him. The love he had for her was shining in his eyes. "I have everything I need."

Epilogue

Sound of Makeda's laughter woke Nyssa from sleep. She must be outside playing in the garden right outside her and Asad's bedroom. Nyssa smiled and reached for her husband, to find his side of the bed empty. Then she hear his laughter and a high shriek from her daughter. Her day had begun. She sat up and grabbed her robe from the end of the bed.

After she tied the sash she walked to the terrace, just in time to see Makeda lobbed a handful of mud at Asad. It hit him in the chest. Makeda pumped her fist in the air and Asad clapped his hand. "A fine toss little queen."

"I told you I could throw."

Makeda was covered in mud, looking more like a girl than the Queen of New Kenya. Nyssa smiled. "What are you two doing playing in the mud like elephants?"

Asad swiped mud off of his cheek and smiled. "We are building you a lotus pond--"

"For my new baby brother," Makeda shouted and threw more mud at Asad. It hit him in face, caking his hair and cheek in the brown ooze.

"How do you know it's a brother?" She rubbed her still flat stomach.

Makeda picked up another handful of mud and threw it at one of Asad's personal guard's but missed. Looking at both stoic men covered in mud, she didn't miss often. "Because Father said it was going to be a boy. And boys are brothers. Although I think I would prefer a sister."

Nyssa stepped barefoot on to the dirt. "The baby needs a lotus pond?"

Asad walked over to her and kissed her cheek. Luckily he didn't get any mud on her. "No My lady, the pond is for you."

"Why do I need a lotus pond?"

His white teeth showed though his muddy smile. "It is tradition."

This she had to hear. "Tell me."

"The lotus closes at night and sinks underwater. In the morning it re-emerges and blooms again. Thus the flower became a natural symbol of the sun and creation and rebirth. Your life has been a series of re-births. We have created a child together. Insuring that the Kuba dynasty will continue to re-born every generation."

A tear prickled her eye. "That's lovely."

Holding up one finger, he said. "But not all."

"The lotus is a symbol of my kingdom in ancient Upper Egypt. The papyrus reeds, which go in the pond is a symbol of Lower Egypt and together in one pond represent the reunification of Upper Africa and Lower Africa."

Oh now she got it. "It's political?"

"No."

She wiped mud off of his cheek. "Why are you building the pond yourself?"

"It is my gift of love for my wife."

Nyssa smiled. She reached up and touched his cheek. She already had her gift. A family.